IN HER COURT

TAMSEN PARKER

In Her Court: © 2017 by Tamsen Parker

Editing by Christa Desir (http://editorchrista.com/)

Copy Editing by Rebecca Weston (http://rawestoneditorial.com)

Cover Design by Lori Carter

ISBN 13: 978-1547105663

For MRF, my favorite geek girl who makes me sound legit.

1

"'Lo?"

"Are you seriously still asleep?"

Willa groaned and rolled over, tempted to silence her phone and throw it across the room for good measure. But Nate would never do that to her, so she rubbed the sleep from her eyes and tried to concentrate. "Clearly not. What's up?"

"You tell me. You never sleep this late. You're always out for a run or whipping up a batch of homemade granola bars or some shit. Are you...? You're not *hungover*, are you?"

Willa groaned again and pulled a pillow over her face. It was too freaking early for Nate's mockingly incredulous tone. "Not unless you count eating a whole pint of Ben and Jerry's as getting wasted."

Nate shouldn't have been able to understand her muffled mutter, but her older brother always seemed to understand her.

"I don't, but you do. You're usually such a health freak with your quinoa and your kale and your—"

With a huff, Willa pushed the pillow off her face. "Is there a point to this or did you just call to mock me? Because I've got to tell you, it's not the best timing."

"Well, you know how you've been depressed since the cave collapse?"

"Yeah, I'm familiar." Hence the Ben and Jerry's binge last night and the sleeping in.

Willa wasn't supposed to be at her crappy graduate student apartment in Stanford; she was supposed to be doing summer fieldwork for her geology program at a newly discovered cavern in Kentucky. Unfortunately, after they'd started work, there'd been a small earthquake and the entrance to the cave had collapsed. It had been at night, so no one had been trapped or hurt, but all their equipment was now stuck inside and there was no telling when they'd be able to get back in, if ever.

It's not as if there weren't other places to do research, but she'd had her heart set on Hendecasyll. Plus, it was halfway through the summer, so finding another place to do research was a no-go. She could read some texts and journals, get more of her references set, but dammit, she'd been looking forward to being out in the world instead of stuck in the library.

"I just so happen to have found you something to do for the rest of the summer."

At that, Willa sat up. "Oh, yeah?"

She'd given up on doing anything terribly productive for the next six weeks or so—there was only so much time a person could spend in the library on a beautiful summer day—and had thought she'd be content to enjoy herself. Wouldn't most people be? She'd only ever been in Stanford as a student, so even though she'd been there for five years so far, she'd never gotten to enjoy all the area had to offer. But instead of doing touristy things on her forced staycation, she'd ended up mostly lying on her couch binge-watching TV she didn't even like, eating crap food she could buy from the convenience store down the street even though there was a perfectly good grocery store a ten-minute bike away, and generally feeling sorry for herself.

It was like a really bad, unexpected breakup. Fucking cave. But Nate knew what she liked, and if he said he had something for her to do, chances were it would not include the phrase *"Would you like fries with that?"*

"Yeah. How would you feel about being a tennis instructor at a camp for grown-ups in the Berkshires?"

Odd. "Isn't that, uh, exactly what you're doing for the summer? Did another camp near you open?"

"No. It's possible Camp Firefly Falls is going to need a replacement instructor."

"Nate. What did you do? Did you sleep with a camper? Get caught doing something inappropriate with a woodland creature? Piss off the owners with paintball graffiti?"

Willa was kind of joking, but kind of not. It would be totally like Nate to take a prank too far and get in deep shit for it. He never quite knew when to quit, which had served him well in school and on the tennis court, but less so other places.

Nate's sniff of insult was clear. "I did nothing of the sort. I'm hurt you would even suggest such a thing. However, it seems likely that I broke my leg."

"What?" Willa tried to reach the lamp on her bedside table and landed on the floor in a heap of blankets instead. She muttered a curse and then turned her attention back to what was actually important. "What do you mean you broke your leg? How? When? Where are you?"

"Slow your roll, Wills. Some of the staff went up to New Hampshire between sessions to do some waterskiing, and—"

"Dammit, Nate."

She and Nate were pretty evenly matched on the tennis court between his strength and her finesse, but she'd always been the one more comfortable in the water. He'd struggled with swimming lessons, but she'd been on the swim team through high school. Plus, grace was not his strong suit. Of course he'd manage to break his leg waterskiing. At least he hadn't drowned.

"So, yeah, I'm calling you from the ER of some Podunk town waiting for an X-ray. I think they're using the machine on a cow or alpaca or something first? Anyway, there's no way I'm going to be able to finish out the summer and I can't stand the idea of sending Heather and Michael scrambling for a replacement. They've got enough on their plates."

Willa was already pulling her suitcase out from under her bed. There wasn't a question involved here. For however much of a dingbat he could be, if Nate said he would do something, he did it. The idea of leaving Heather and Michael in the lurch probably hurt more than his leg did, and she could understand that. Their parents had drilled responsibility into them from an early age, and it had stuck. "We Show Up" was practically the Carter family motto.

Nate needed her. Even though he was an enormous doofus and this was clearly his own damn fault and she was angry at him for burying the lede, he was still her big brother, and he'd drop anything and everything to do her a solid if their positions were reversed.

Plus, she could still do most of her reading at camp—almost all the journals she needed were online—and not moping around feeling sorry for herself would make her more productive. She liked being busy, and this way she could run the court during the day and read at night, a perfect combination of her two loves.

"Next time you break a limb, maybe start with that and then make me a job offer? But, yes, I'll book a flight. Did you already call Mom and Dad? What's the closest airport?"

Once they'd worked out the details, Nate plied her with more gratitude. "You're the best, Wills. I'm totally going to make this up to you."

Willa had popped over to her laptop to look at flights online when she remembered a tiny, insignificant detail. "Where's Van? Wasn't this supposed to be three months of you guys making friendship bracelets and building campfires?"

Nate worked for one of those uber-cool robotics start-ups that had sick employee benefits like unlimited vacation time. He was taking advantage of that particular perk to be at camp this summer with his bestie—though knowing what a workaholic he was, he was probably spending as much time on his laptop and with his soldering kit as he was teaching lessons.

"Van didn't come water skiing. If you recall, she has better sense than I do." Willa bit back the *Yeah, who doesn't?* she wanted to say. Nate had a broken leg, and his pride probably hurt worse than his injury. She should take it easy on him. "Also, she only sort of took the summer off because that's all she could manage. She's still at camp, catching up on some stuff with her job. Why do you ask?"

"No reason." Nope, no reason at all. Aside from the fact Willa had had a crush on Van since sometime in the third grade. Maybe it was when Van had fixed the elevator in her Barbie Dream House or when she'd rescued Willa's favorite My Little Pony from being used as BB gun target practice. Yeah, she'd basically always had a thing for her brother's best friend.

"Van will be excited to see you. It's been—what, ten years?"

Eight, since Van and Nate had graduated from college, but who was counting? Oh, wait, Willa was. Van and Nate had gone to different grad schools, and while Van and Nate had stayed almost freakishly close, Van had ceased to be a fixture at the Carter home, much to Willa's dismay.

"She always thought you were freaking adorable."

And therein lay the problem. Willa didn't want to be adorable. She wanted Van to think she was smart, cool, and dammit if she were being totally honest, sexy. Because that's how Willa had always thought of Van, and she couldn't imagine much had changed in the intervening years. With the snippets she'd caught of Van from Nate's social media, Van enthralled her as much as she always had.

Van had a certain sense of style—half mad-scientist, half-Diane Keaton circa *Annie Hall*. She should've looked ridiculous—and god knew Willa would if she tried to pull that look off—but on Van, it was…well, it was lip-bite-inducing.

Add in her crazy-brilliant brain that worked in ways Willa would never understand and her quirky sense of humor, and Willa was a goner. Total and utter puddle of girl-crush goo. For someone who was totally out of her league. Which was why she'd never bothered to connect with Van on any social media. It would be beyond humiliating to have her request rejected. Even if Van accepted, she'd feel like it was a pity friending and that might be worse, so she'd settled for cyber-stalking through Nate.

Maybe if Van could see her now, she'd see Willa wasn't the same blonde moppet who used to trail after them. She was a strong, intelligent, and pretty freaking attractive woman who had her own life and ambitions. Really, if Van had any sense, she'd be the one chasing after Willa by the end of the summer…

Nate's voice interrupted her daydreams. "At least you won't have to bunk with a stranger. You can have mine in the cabin I was sharing with Van."

"Great," she said weakly. And by great, she meant fan-freaking-tastic. Nothing like spending the rest of the summer with a smoking hot woman who would pat her on the head like a puppy. Nate was damn lucky she adored him.

———

"Nathaniel Leichtensteinium Carter—"

"Van, that's not my name, and you know it."

She'd like to throttle Nate, but even she hadn't figured ou

how to defy the laws of physics in order to do that through a cell connection. Apparently she'd be settling for giving him a serious amount of shit.

"You don't have a middle name, which is flat-out vexing. You could've had a perfectly reasonable multisyllabic first name, but noooo. Nate. Did your mother not realize how exasperating you were going to be and how satisfying it would be to grind out your full name between her teeth? Nate Carter is far too short for such purposes."

Van slammed her laptop shut and started pacing her small office at the main lodge. Being the camp's web presence manager and all around IT minion wasn't the most glamorous position, and the closet they'd essentially assigned her wasn't luxe by any means, but at least it was hers. Which was decent for a temporary, part-time gig. Plus, it gave her a place where she could pace like a crazy person and not have anyone look at her like she was losing her mind.

"Not like Evangeline Anastasia Thompson?"

"Exactly. Now that's a name you can sink your teeth into. With plenty of opportunities to raise your voice with emphasis. Now shut up. I can't believe you're ditching out on me. We were supposed to have all summer, and now you're leaving? That blows, man."

Van had committed to this camp job last year. Nate had signed on to be the tennis instructor, and when Heather mentioned to him she was looking for a dedicated IT person because handling it all herself was overwhelming, he'd told her he knew just the person for the job.

Van had agreed, thinking it would be fun to spend a summer with Nate, but after the shit-tacular year she'd had as her first year as a professor, it had become a lifeboat she couldn't wait to sail away on. And now her first mate was jumping ship. Or her captain, really, because this whole thing had been Nate's idea in the first place.

Van hated when people backed out of things they had committed to. In all fairness, Nate had a pretty valid excuse and he'd built up a lifetime of goodwill of being where he was supposed to be when he was supposed to be there, but his abandonment still poked a sore spot.

"I know, and I'm sorry you have such a moron for a best friend. If it makes you feel any better, my leg really hurts."

Van grunted and picked up her trusty Rubik's cube. Some of the colors were rubbing off. She'd have to take the Sharpies to it again. "That only makes me feel a little better. Seriously, though, why'd you get Willa to come? The only thing worse than not having you here is having to babysit your kid sister for the rest of the summer. I don't do well with children."

Or with jocks. The only thing Willa had seemed to take seriously when they were growing up was her tennis game. Yeah, she'd worked hard at it and Van had a grudging respect for her dedication, but Willa had never seemed to have much use for intellectual pursuits, so they'd never found much to talk about. Van couldn't imagine things had changed much.

She wouldn't know for a fact. She loved Nate, but she only had so much room in her head for social niceties. Birthdays, babies, moving, new jobs—they pretty much went in one ear and out the other. Unless you were one of Van's people, she didn't even attempt to keep track of those details, and that did not extend to family.

"For starters, Willa's not much younger than us. She's twenty-three, not exactly in need of a babysitter. Why does none of this stick with you? Besides, if you don't want to keep an eye on her I'm sure one of the other single staffers would be happy to. don't want to sound gross because she's my sister, but I have it on good authority Willa's pretty hot."

"Ew, dude. That *is* gross."

"Whatever. I'm just saying, she's not going to be tagging along after you for the next six weeks, I promise."

Van stopped her pacing long enough to put down her Rubik's cube and pick up a wad of slime from her desk. She threw the green…stuff against the wall, and it made a satisfying splat and then proceeded to slip down the wood. That probably wouldn't leave a mark, but she should take it off just in case.

"Fine. But you better tell her I don't want to deal with socks on the cabin door or waking up next to some snoring dudebro, okay? They can keep that shit in the woods where it belongs."

"I'll tell her, although lately she's been dating more women than men."

She peeled off the goo and swore. "I changed my mind. Babysitting some pig-tailed little girl would surely be better than having some baby dyke hanging on me. Nate, I'm going to kill you."

"Well, on my crutches, you might actually be able to catch me."

Van ran a hand through the hair that had flopped in front of her face during her manic pacing and looked for something to punch that wouldn't break her hand. Nothing being convenient, she threw the slime against the wall again. "You suck, Carter."

"It's not my fault you value academic pursuits over the physical. If you hit the gym once in a while instead of locking yourself in your lab, you'd have a better shot."

No, what she'd have would be a tighter ass and no tenure-track position, maybe not even a completed postdoc or a PhD. No thank you. Although at this point, she was starting to question the wisdom of that decision. But that was because she was coming up on the start of her real, actual career. Not just all the boxes she'd had to check off on the way there—straight-A student in high school with a shit ton of science, math, and engineering extracurriculars; an undergrad with a four point nine GPA; a couple of lab assistant-ships at the most prestigious technical university in the world; a PhD from the same school; and letters of recommendation from literal Nobel prizewinners in her field—but the end game.

No one worked harder or deserved a tenure-track position at a top university like Van did. And dammit, she was going to claim it and not let the equivalent of wedding day jitters scare her off. Besides, sticking with things was a point of pride for her. She wouldn't abandon something just because the going got a little rough.

"Yeah, well, I can still build a robot that can hunt you down, steal your crutches, and beat you with them." Yes, her PhD was in physics, but she'd taken some electrical engineering classes for fun during college and had gotten into robotics because she wanted to be able to talk to Nate about his life's work. Besides, everyone needed a hobby.

"Of that I have no doubt, but surely you've got better things to do?"

Picking up her Rubik's cube again, Van dropped into the squeaky office chair and spun around, stopping herself by resting her crossed ankles on her desk.

"Like pack up your shit and make room for my new bunkmate?"

"You better be nice to Willa. No hazing allowed, okay? No short-sheeting her bed, no bleach in her shampoo bottle. She does not appreciate pranks, and you'd hurt her feelings if you pulled that shit. I know you and your family aren't close, but love Willa and her happiness means a lot to me."

"Fine."

"I don't believe you, Van."

Ugh, Nate's tone was a verbal wagging finger. But she had to admit there was a good reason for that. Van was still tempted to drive little Willa Carter out of the cabin with some plastic spiders under her pillow. Maybe the mess of Van's clothes spilling out of the closet would be enough?

"I'll be good, okay?"

"Swear on Holtzmann."

Van stopped fidgeting with her Rubik's cube, even though she was only a few moves away from getting all the squares where they belonged.

"Which one?" Van's gaze combed over the multitude of *Ghostbusters* stickers and pins decorating the bulletin board, the figurines lining the back of her desk, the goggles dangling from the bookshelf. But she knew which one Nate meant. Jerkface.

"You know which one I'm talking about. Your mint-condition action figure with the box signed by Kate McKinnon. You paid a small fortune for that thing. Even more than that old-school, limited-edition Wonder Woman LEGO set."

Some people had pictures of their children; she had action figures and didn't Nate know exactly how much she loved them. In fact, preferred them to most people because they never did anything unexpected. Their behavior was predictable, consistent, and reliable. Just how she liked things and just how she'd arranged her life for as long as she'd been the one doing the arranging.

"You play dirty, Nathanderson Quigglesville Carter."

"You only say that because I know what's actually important to you. We should be back to camp around six, and we can have one last night before I go home, okay? Surely beer will only have amazing effects on my pain meds."

"I'll pull the good stuff out and get it in the fridge," she grumbled and then hung up, because she and Nate had never been much for goodbyes. It was a given: they'd talk later. The longest they'd gone without communicating in some fashion was when Nate had gone to tennis camp during the summers when they

were kids. That month had always been the longest of Van'
childhood years.

But unlike those Julys, when she'd stare at her poster-covered
walls and make list upon list of all the things they could do
together when he got back, he wouldn't be coming back to camp
She'd have to make do with the lesser Carter for the rest of the
summer. Before he abandoned her, he'd return in a few hours, so
she'd better get back to the cabin and box up the stuff he
wouldn't need tonight. *Dammit, Nate.*

2

ABOUT FOUR HOURS LATER, Van had managed to clean up the cabin. As much as she was willing to clean up the cabin at any rate—tidiness had never been one of her virtues. Nate's things were packed up in the duffel bags and milk crates he'd brought, because despite being a grown man with a master's degree and an engineer's salary, he still lived like an undergrad.

The Carters lived not so far away and were the kind of parents who actually enjoyed being parents and seemed to miss Nate and Willa now they'd left home, so they were going to drop Willa off tomorrow morning, pick Nate up, and bring him back to their house in Connecticut—the house that had been a second home to Van growing up too. He'd leave his Subaru for Willa to use while she was here—it wasn't as though Nate could drive with his busted-up leg anyhow.

Lucky for him, his parents still lived in the house he and Willa had grown up in and had no intention of leaving. Van's parents had retired to Florida years ago and never came north if they could help it—even Charlottesville counted as north. If something like this had happened to her, she'd be on her own. As much as she was ever on her own, she supposed. Nate was always there. He would totally fly down from Boston to get her settled and entertained for as long as he could if she got hurt or sick.

Except now he'd be abandoning her and leaving her alone but with his baby sister. Willa had been cute as a kid, but she wasn't a kid anymore. What had she been doing that she could drop it and fill in for Nate as a tennis instructor anyway? Probably lolling around being blonde, because that's what it seemed like a lot of those country club types did over the summers. Worked on their tans.

That wasn't entirely fair, though, because the Carters were nothing if not devoted to each other. Even if she'd been doing something important or that she loved, Willa likely would've dropped it to come help Nate out. It was what that family did, and Van conceded to some begrudging respect to Willa. At least the two of them would have that much in common: an allegiance to Nate.

Van was about to settle down on her bunk with the latest issue of *Wonder Woman* while she waited for Nate to hobble through the door. Instead, her email pinged. And not just any ping. The cheery one that had come to feel ominous since it was from her university email. It probably wasn't a good sign that every time she heard that sound she rolled her eyes, groaned, or covered her eyes with whatever was handy. Hat, pillow, comic book. All of the above. Sometimes she wanted to bury herself and then she'd have an excuse not to go to work anymore, because she'd be dead. She could picture her obituary now:

Van Thompson, pre-eminent professor of computational biophysics at the University of Virginia, passed away last week. She was crushed by the weight of her science-fiction and superhero memorabilia collections. She is survived by her parents, a brother, two sisters, and of course, Holtzmann.

For something she'd wanted so badly for so long, her job sure was something she avoided like the plague. The truth was, she loathed being a professor. University politics were insane, the students were a mixed bag at best—she wanted to set 90 percent of her intro lecture section on fire—and the pressure to publish and get grants was out of control.

But Van Thompson wasn't a quitter. Her parents had quit every business they'd started because they grew bored of them and had also only shown up about two out of three times they'd said they would, which had driven Van up the wall as a kid. Ever since she could swear, she'd sworn up and down she wouldn't be like them.

Sure, she recognized some things were strengths and some weaknesses, but she could almost always avoid doing anything that would showcase her weaknesses and she wouldn't commit to something if she wasn't going to show up. Organized sports, for example, were entirely a no-go. Which was because she knew herself.

And what she knew right now was she did not want to look at the latest email from the university, but she probably should.

Digging the phone out of her pocket, she opened the email. It was from her department head and was about fall semester scheduling. Maybe they'd decided to let her teach a class in advanced simulation techniques for biomolecules after all? That would be awesome. It might only have limited appeal, but the subject matter was so rich, and for the right students, it would be crazy compelling. She bet she could recruit a few more majors if they'd—

Fuck. She should've known better. They weren't accepting her proposal for a new course. They were asking her to pick up another intro lecture because one of the more senior professors in the department—aka, anyone—wanted to teach yet another section of computational methods for physics. Fuck that shit.

Thankfully, before she could lose her mind and write back

some scathing reply that would no doubt have her out on her ass, something banged at the door and she could hear prolific cursing on the other side. Nate was back.

So she shook her head, trying to get her adolescent angsting out, and went to let him in before he broke something else.

———

Was it humanly possible for the older generation of Carters not to drive a Volvo? Van swore for the entirety of her acquaintance with them, ever since she was a kid, they'd had a long parade of station wagons—she'd ridden in every single one of them—and this was no different.

And though his hair was somewhat greyer than she remembered, Mr. Carter was easily recognizable as he slid out from behind the driver's seat and smiled at her.

"Van! It's been a long time. How's my favorite physicist doing?"

He slung an arm around her shoulders and squeezed briefly before letting her go. She knew the Carters couldn't help themselves—they were wired for casual affection—but she'd always found it a bit alarming. Other people she might tell to get the fuck off, but she'd spent more time with the Carters than she had at her own house growing up. They'd always let her be herself without demanding or expecting apologies, so the least she could do was try not to get twitchy over the occasional physical contact.

"Good, Mr. Carter. But do you even know any other physicists?" He was an intellectual property rights lawyer who specialized in the arts, so she doubted it. You never knew with the Carters, though. They attracted a motley crew—clearly.

Mr. Carter waved a finger at her. "Good point. But I think even if I knew a dozen, you'd still be my favorite."

Van's cheeks got warm at the compliment. It was so easy for them, wasn't it? To give away approval and fondness like that. Despite all the time she'd spent over the years with the Carters, it had never rubbed off on her. She was still as stiff and awkward as ever, but they didn't seem to mind.

She didn't have to respond, though, because Mrs. Carter was there in her white capri pants and a blue-and-white striped shirt. She always looked…clean. Neat. Even though her tan and the baskets of produce she regularly unloaded on Nate said she must spend half her time out of doors.

"Van, darling, how are you?" The greeting was accompanied by a brief hug and a quick buss to her cheek Van tried to accept gracefully.

"Good, thanks, Mrs. Carter. How are you?"

"Well, I'd prefer it if my son would stop breaking limbs…" She rolled her eyes and gave Van an affectionately exasperated look, and Van responded with a nod as she was supposed to. Mrs. Carter had often treated her as a coconspirator, but Van's loyalty lay squarely with Nate, whatever stupid shit he might pull. Despite that, she'd learned it was easiest to agree with Mrs. C. That woman was tenacious. "But it's a good excuse to get our Willa back on the East Coast."

Then she was there. Or, at least, Van thought it was Willa. Van hadn't seen her in person since she and Nate had graduated from college, and that had been eight years ago. Willa had always been pretty in a girl-in-a-catalogue way, but the woman who was standing in front of her, arm draped over her mother's shoulders, wasn't pretty.

She was a knockout.

Even travel-worn and, Van would imagine, sleep-deprived since she'd taken a red-eye to get here, Willa looked amazing. She had on one of those short-sleeved tunic dresses Van wouldn't be caught dead in and some strappy sandals that showed off her feet and ankles and, yeah, her legs. Damn those Carter siblings for their athletic prowess. They got all the breaks: looks, loving family, athleticism, and a better-than-average amount of brains in their heads.

Girls were always hitting on Nate when they went out, and she couldn't imagine Willa suffered fewer amorous attentions, what with that body. Was it fair someone who worked out so much should still have breasts like that? No, no, it was not fair. She'd definitely earned those cut arms though.

Nate had said Willa was—what, twenty-three? No matter she was well above legal, Van shouldn't be staring at her like she was an item on the menu. She was Nate's little sister for god's sake.

As such, she had that trademark easy Carter smile. Coming from Nate and the elder Carters, it made her feel welcome and warm, but coming from Willa... Warm was not going to cover it. Made her want to pull at her collar. "Hey, Van. It's been a while. I hear we're going to be bunkmates."

Shit, yes, bunkmates.

Say something, Thompson, and not something about how hot she is. "Yep."

Way to go. Luckily, no one seemed to expect her to be terribly articulate. That was the beauty of having done research in a field as specific as simulating the folding of minimalist protein models. Everyone expected her to be nerdy and awkward and to barely speak English. The Carters knew somewhat better, but even they didn't expect her to be a social butterfly.

Van stared at the picture-perfect Carters for a minute before it occurred to her she was the expert here. Being an expert was something she could handle.

"I'll show you how to get to the cabin. I left Nate there since he's not so great with the crutches yet."

This plan also afforded Van the advantage of being able to turn her back on Willa so Willa couldn't see all the panicked and aroused thoughts her presence was stirring up. Van had been worried about having Willa tag after her or trying to earn some queer cred by hanging out with a Real Actual Lesbian™. Now, however, she was far more concerned about not making a fool out of her own damn self.

3

WELL. Van Thompson was much as she remembered. Quirky, awkward, and yeah, really fucking hot. She wasn't wearing glasses right now—maybe contacts?—but Willa had every hope she would be soon. The outfit Van had on shouldn't have worked, and probably wouldn't have on anyone else, but on her it was nothing short of magical.

High-waisted pants emphasized the flare of Van's hips, and they were topped with suspenders fastened over a sleeveless button-down. Willa envied Van's ability to wear a button-down—damn things always gaped in a wildly inappropriate way on her—and surely that was the only reason she found her gaze drawn to Van's chest. Not that she was contemplating exactly what was under her shirt.

Willa forced her attention to the badass Wonder Woman Chucks that were rapidly moving down the path toward the cabin she'd be sharing with Van for...what had Nate said? Six weeks left of camp?

It was going to be torture if the past two minutes were any indication.

She followed Van through the wooded clusters of cabins,

listening to her parents chatter back and forth about their plans for the weekend. Apparently they were going to some big antique fair and then golfing with the Mitchells, and on Sunday, after her mother did her weeding, they were supposed to go to a concert at Tanglewood because they were the world's most perfect retired couple.

Seeing them always made her wonder if she'd be able to find someone who she wanted to grow old with and what that person might be like. She had some ideas, but as any scientist worth their salt knew, hypotheses and realities didn't always mesh.

Nate was standing—or really, slumping—at the door to the cabin. Van had been right about him not being down with the crutches yet. He hobbled onto the porch and looked as though he might fall down the stairs. Luckily her father waved Nate back into the cabin he'd called home for the beginning of the summer and where she would stay through the end.

"Don't make it worse, tiger. You've had your mother fretting enough."

Nate laughed and shook his head, but did as he was told, managing to go into the small building without another incident that would require a trip to an ER. Then went Van, followed by her parents, and last, Willa with a duffel bag full of tennis clothes and shoes and bathing suits and sunscreen that she proceeded to drop on what was clearly her side of the room.

Van had never been a neat freak, and some things never changed. Neither had Nate, who nearly tripped her with a crutch as he dumped himself into a desk chair. "Welcome to Camp Firefly Falls, sis. May you break fewer limbs than I have."

———

ONCE HER PARENTS, Nate, and all of Nate's stuff were on their way back to the house in Fairfield, Willa set to putting her things away on her side of the cabin. It wasn't a big space, nor was it particularly luxurious, but it was fun that way. It was like being back at the tennis camp she and Nate had gone to every summer, except here she and Van had a bathroom to themselves. They wouldn't have to haul ass in the morning to the shower shed to relieve themselves.

Thank goodness, because there had been some freaky shit in the shower sheds, like giant moths attracted by the lights that stayed on all night and the occasional raccoon who'd gotten stuck in a trash bin. Even better, she wouldn't have to share with dozens of girls and their innumerable toiletries. Just Van, who she suspected was a minimalist when it came to primping.

Yep, she didn't think she'd have to fight with Van for valuable shelf space in the shower or towel hooks. Maybe who got to take a shower when, because they would have to share that every day. Which also meant Van would be naked on the other side of that flimsy door.

Not okay, Carter. Keep your eye on the ball. Be friendly.

Willa set a picture of her family on vacation at the Grand Canyon on her dresser. "So Nate told me you finished up your first year as a professor at UVA in May. How'd that go?"

Van blinked at her, as if she was surprised to be addressed. She'd always been owlish, looking a bit taken aback anyone other than Nate would want to converse with her.

"Fine."

Willa waited for more, but it never came. Van had never been super-chatty, but when asked a direct question, especially about something she was presumably passionate about, she could be counted on to muster more than a one-word answer. And yet...

Yep, these six weeks were going to be interminable. She was curious, though, and—while she didn't let on to hardly anyone about this—somewhat concerned about her own prospects in academia. So she pressed, hoping Van would perk up and have something to say. Give them something to bond over and maybe even make Willa feel better about being able to hack a PhD and then hopefully become a professor. "Are you super-psyched to have a tenure-track position? Those are getting harder to come by all the time."

Indeed, Willa was painfully aware of the reality. Geology and physics weren't exactly comparable, and Van was far more of an academic badass than Willa had ever been or would ever be, but still. She knew she had an uphill battle ahead of her if she wanted to be a professor, and maybe Van could inspire her.

"I suppose."

Willa set out another picture and then turned fully toward Van, resting her hands on the edge of the dresser. This was a rather awkward conversation even for Van. Plus, it's not as if she was trying to talk to Van about the US Open or some other thing she didn't give a shit about. Academics were Van's life. Well, outside of her love for all things Wonder Woman, *Ghostbusters*, and *Star Wars* at any rate.

"Well, I was hoping you might be able to give me some pointers. After I finish up with my PhD, I'm hoping to get a job in academia too."

At that, Van's head snapped up from where she'd been studying the pattern on her socks. "What?"

"Yeah, um, maybe Nate didn't tell you?" *Or maybe you didn't care to ask?* "I started a PhD in geology. First year down…a million to go."

Well, probably more like four or five, depending on how her research went, but given that a good chunk of her research time had been scrapped because of that stupid cave collapse—

and she might have to reconsider the topic of her dissertation altogether if she couldn't find a new site to do research at—it was looking longer and longer.

Willa expected at least a smile from Van; she'd found fellow advanced degree-seekers or holders to be endlessly willing and able to complain about academia, despite being grateful for it at the end of the day. Instead, she got a wrinkled nose and a "Why?"

"Why?" Willa echoed.

"Yeah, why? Because I've got to tell you, academia's not all it's cracked up to be. It's fucking miserable if you want to know the truth. Besides, wouldn't you rather be, I don't know, playing tennis or something?"

Right. Because she was a dumb jock. "No, actually."

She probably could've turned pro, with luck and timing, but the more she'd played at the college level, the less she had wanted to play tennis for a living. The insane amount of pressure sucked the fun out of the game. Whereas some people were energized by it, Willa had found it draining. She'd ended up retreating into her books and into the major she'd specifically chosen because it was supposed to be easy. They didn't call Geology 101 Rocks for Jocks just because it rhymed.

But as things so often happen, one thing had led to another and she'd fallen in love. With rocks. More specifically with caves and the formations within them: speleothems. Such a clunky name for such elegant things. Who knew that in addition to the things science hadn't figured out about space or deep in the sea that there were still mysteries to be solved in the very earth upon which they walked? So freaking cool.

So she'd applied to grad programs at a few different schools but had been pretty excited that she'd been able to stay at Stanford.

Willa waited in hopes maybe Van would apologize—say she was irritated with department politics or she hadn't been awarded a grant she'd applied for, had a paper rejected from a journal she had her eyes on, or some other given frustration of academic life—but it didn't come. Fine.

She had better things to do. Like eat and then meet up with

Heather, the camp director who would be her boss, but who Nate had also said she'd likely get along with. A good thing too because apparently she and her bunkmate weren't going to be bosom buddies.

"Well, I think I'll go grab some lunch before the dining lodge closes."

Van acknowledged her with a half-assed wave and no eye contact.

While Willa should've been annoyed, she was more sad. It had been one thing to be rejected by Nate and Van when they were kids and she was small and—now she could admit—totally not prepared to join their games. Seven years when they were kids had seemed like an insurmountable difference. Now, though, it didn't seem like such a big deal. Plus, being blown off as a grown-up by someone who she both admired and found attractive? That was the pits, especially since she'd have to see Van every freaking day for the next six weeks. Maybe this camp thing hadn't been such a great idea after all.

4

WHY THE TENNIS courts needed to be between the cabins and the main lodge where her office was was beyond Van. When Nate had been here, it had seemed like good luck: they would walk to breakfast together, and if Van wasn't urgently needed, she'd head back to the cabin and drop Nate off on the way. If Heather was freaking out about something or there was something better done first thing, then she'd stay in her office doing a report on the efficacy of their online advertising or getting the next round of surveys set up or one of her hundred other small duties until lunch. Then she'd meet Nate and walk him back by the courts for his afternoon lessons. Perfect.

Now the tennis courts seemed like a black hole she only narrowly avoided being sucked into. Because whenever she walked by, who was there but Willa? Either bashing a ball against the self-play wall, teaching some lucky person how to hold a racquet, or playing against her students, doing that funny thing of shouting out instructions on how to beat her. Of course, they rarely did, even with that advantage.

Day after day, Van passed and tried not to stare too hard at her bunkmate and those ridiculously sexy tennis outfits of hers.

They showed off Willa's broad shoulders, her muscular biceps, and her defined forearms. Not to mention her legs. The woman's legs were…out of control. Strong and shapely, and goddammit, they made her look statuesque even when she was drinking out of a plastic water bottle. And the times Willa was in motion when Van passed by—surreptitiously watching her move lest she be seriously busted for perving on her bunkmate, not to mention Nate's younger sister—she looked like a lithe jungle cat. A jungle cat with a really fantastic ass.

Today was one of those days when Heather hadn't needed her first thing, so Van had spent the morning in her cabin trying to get a grant proposal written. After she'd pretended to be asleep while Willa got ready for the day, of course.

Even as she was doing it, she cursed herself. Not only would it be ridiculous and embarrassing if Willa ever realized it, but it was also inefficient. Van could've been doing so many things, and the knowledge chafed as surely as a wool sweater. But her fear overwhelmed even the practical part of her.

Being around women she found attractive had a way of making her stupid, which was pretty much the only reason she was thankful her profession was still male-dominated. It was easy to work around dudes, because no matter how intelligent, how objectively attractive, how charming or funny, they did absolutely squat for her libido.

Willa, on the other hand, did just about everything for her. Even before she'd said she was getting a PhD, Van had been gone on her looks. She'd never thought much about how smart Willa was, partly because Willa had seemed to care more about her tennis game. But apparently, she was hot *and* had brains, which was an enormous problem.

So Van had been handling it how she usually did—by avoiding Willa like the plague. Which was awkward since they lived together, but she would much rather Willa think she was a dick than ruin her friendship with Nate over what would likely be a fling, if anything at all, with his beloved baby sister. Since she hadn't kept up with Willa, she really had no idea if she was even Willa's type.

Van was aware she wasn't super-hot, which was fine. She was relatively pleased by the way she looked, and honestly, being attractive seemed to be far more trouble than it was worth. She also didn't have a ton of money because academia wasn't particularly lucrative, especially in the early years. The response of women she'd been to bed with seemed to indicate she was a decent lover, but given the sample size, she could only call the evidence anecdotal. Which left brains as her most attractive feature.

Van's Chucks crunched down the path; she'd timed her trip to the dining lodge very carefully. After lunch had begun—so she'd be unlikely to catch Willa on the court and have to endure the torture of seeing her crush at Willa's most attractive—but also not so late that she would miss out on the best selections. Over the past week or so, she'd perfected her timing.

Unfortunately, Willa's behavior was far more erratic than Van's own and the cursed woman had foiled her plans once again. There she was, bouncing on the balls of her feet, waiting to receive her opponent's serve. And when it came, there she went, moving at some crazy speed that should've been beyond a human. It jolted something inside Van and she nearly tripped over her own feet.

Really, what else was she supposed to do when a sudden fantasy of her biggest crush cosplaying as Wonder Woman seized her as effectively as the golden lasso? Dammit. Of course Willa's opponent—who it seemed was actually Heather—couldn't get to her return because Willa was insane, so she wasn't distracted enough by playing not to notice Van.

No, instead, she stood there, gold tendrils of hair that had escaped from her high ponytail curling around her exertion-pinked face, and waved. "Hey, Van."

Not even trusting her own voice, Van waved in what she hoped was a perfectly normal way and then looked down at her feet so she wouldn't trip on a rock and face-plant in front of Willa. Also, she didn't want to be too late to lunch because there were lobster rolls today, and Meg made killer lobster rolls. A balm made out of arthropod, mayo, celery, and a buttered roll. If anything could soothe the rawness from her plan not working and having to interact with Willa unexpectedly, it would be that.

———

WILLA WIPED the sweat from her hairline and stared after Van. Stared until the person on the other side of the court cleared her throat.

"Uh, Willa?"

She shook her head and turned back to the net where Heather was standing, racquet and ball in her hands. "Yeah, sorry."

Willa jogged back to the baseline and Heather headed to her own. Once there, Willa reminded Heather of the basics: stand between the center mark and the singles line, but behind the baseline, and aim for the opposite service box. That was plenty for now; she'd convey more strategy when Heather was able to get it over the net and into the service box consistently. Which didn't seem like it was in danger of happening today.

They played for a while longer, and Willa enjoyed herself. Not that Heather was a true adversary, but she was easy to talk to, and given that she was living with the Queen of the Monosyllables, the change was welcome. Heather told her about how she'd come to resurrect Camp Firefly Falls and, in the process of doing so, had resurrected her marriage. The story had Willa so swoony she actually failed to return one of Heather's serves.

After about twenty minutes more, though, Heather excused herself because she was supposed to meet Michael for lunch and didn't want to miss out on the lobster rolls. As delicious as that sounded, it wasn't comfort food. That's what Willa needed right now: comfort. She wasn't used to doubting herself, but Van's behavior had her off her game.

Once she and Heather had parted ways, Willa drew her cell out of her bag and pressed one of her speed dial buttons.

"Please don't tell me you're calling from the Briarsted drunk tank."

"Oh my god, Nate. A) It's not even one in the afternoon—"

"Yeah, but it's always five o'clock somewhere." It sounded like it might be five o'clock in Fairfield actually—had her mother been spiking the lemonade again? That's just what Nate needed.

"B) I have a lesson in half an hour; and C) Why do you know there's a drunk tank in Briarsted?"

Nate laughed, and yeah, she was pretty sure he'd been drowning his sorrows in their mom's grown-up lemonade or a pitcher of Tipsy Arnies—her mother's take on the Arnold Palmer, which included limoncello and elderflower liqueur for good measure, because Georgina Carter was basically the WASPiest person on the planet.

"I'm just joshing you, Wills. Because I am bored as fuck."

"So you're getting plastered to entertain yourself?"

"I've been with Mom and Dad for almost two weeks. You'd be hitting the bottle too."

So true. She loved her parents to death, but they could be a bit much. Especially when they were still so happy after being married since dinosaurs roamed the Earth. It was nice and adorable, yes, but also a reminder that neither she nor Nate had found someone. Though he'd never admit it, she suspected it hit Nate harder since he was thirty to her twenty-three.

"Fair."

"So if you're not calling for me to bail you out, what's up? How's camp? Are you and Heather besties yet?"

"I wouldn't say besties, but yeah, Heather's pretty cool. My students are good, the activities have been fun, and I like our cabin."

"But?"

Yeah, *but*. Nate could always suss out when she was unhappy, and it wasn't worth trying to wriggle out of it. Even drunk off his gourd, he'd know and he'd hunt her down when he was sober and demand she tell him what was up. Better to do it now while she had some privacy on the walk back to her cabin.

"I think Van hates me."

"Van doesn't hate you."

Willa felt the strong urge to stick her tongue out at the phone. "Would you even tell me if she did? I don't think so."

"Mmm, probably not in so many words because I've been told that's rude..." That earned an eye roll. Classic Nate. Only realizing something was an issue when he'd been smacked upside the head with it. At least once he had been, he wouldn't do it again, which was more than she could say for some people. "But there's no way Van hates you. You guys are my two best girls. Don't tell Van I said that because she'll punch me the next time I see her, but it's true. So she can't hate you."

"That doesn't make any sense. Just because you think something is true doesn't mean it's so."

Nate made a disgruntled noise, followed by a crude slurping sound and then him bellowing in her ear. "Mom! I'm out!"

"Yeah, because you clearly need another," Willa muttered. "It's fine. Forget I mentioned it. But she barely says a word to me, and I feel like she avoids me whenever possible, and I don't think I did anything, but I also don't know that Van and I occupy the same plane of reality, so maybe I did something unacceptable and I don't even know it?"

"Look. Geeks are a different subculture, but they're not a different species. I know you. I know Van. There's nothing between you that would make you neme...nemesesses? Nemeses?"

Okay, so even though he was drunk, calling Nate had been a good idea. He might not be able to give her advice, but at least he'd made her laugh. "Nemeses. I'm probably overreacting. Van's not one for chatter. I thought maybe we could be friends, that's all. I don't want to poach her from you—not that I could—but it should be nice having someone I know here, and instead, it's weird."

"I don't know what to tell you, Wills. Just keep enjoying the enjoyable stuff and tell Van to jump in the lake. That's what I would do."

He wasn't kidding. Knowing Nate, he'd probably take it further and bodily deposit Van in said lake. "You're smarter than you look, Nate Carter."

"Thanks. Hey, wait a second, that was a—"

Willa hung up, giggling, before Nate could get in another word and gave herself a high-five, wondering how long it would take him to figure out she'd hung up.

5

"'Sup?"

"Do you always answer the phone like that?"

If she said yes, Nate would probably believe her. She knew she wasn't the queen of social graces or anything, but she was better than that. Slightly. "Only when I know it's you."

"Should I be flattered? And what are you… Are you eating?"

"Yep."

"Your phone manners are atrocious."

She crunched down on another chip and put her feet up on the desk. This was going to take a while. "You're lucky I let you see my true colors, Nathanuel Remingsfield Carter."

"Seriously, dude, can you chill on the snacking for the five minutes this conversation is going to take? And then you can get back to eating your…"

"Pringles," Van filled in, her mouth still full of the crunchy, salty goodness.

"It's not even nine o'clock yet. What the hell are you doing eating potato chips?"

"A) Pringles are not just any potato chip. They are by far the pinnacle of potato-chip-hood with their delightful parabola shape and their innovative packaging which greatly reduces the incidence of greasy fingers and crushed chips at the bottom like those inferior bags. B) They ran out of Hyper O's in the dining lodge by the time I got there, and you know I require crunch in the morning."

She ignored Nate's grumbled protest about eating a slice of toast like a normal person and proceeded to complete her list.

"And C) If they're good enough for Holtzmann, they're good enough for me."

"Sure, whatever. Give me a minute, okay?"

Van obediently placed the tube on her desk and picked up a fidget cube. It was the yellow one, her favorite. She was in a spinning mood, so she thumbed the small disc on one side around and around and around. "Fine. What do you want?"

"You're making Willa unhappy, and you know how I feel about that."

Not good. Nate did not feel good about people making Willa unhappy. But Van wasn't willing to cop to this yet. "Did she tell you she was unhappy?"

"She's not, for the most part. She loves Heather, she's enjoying her students, and she likes being at camp. So, actually, she's having a pretty great time."

"Then I'm not sure what the—"

"Except for you, Van. What the hell?"

"What?" The spinning was no longer cutting it. Clicking was definitely required for this conversation. She wasn't great with people. She knew that, and she'd come to terms with it. Being a social butterfly and having gobs of friends wasn't her jam. Having a couple of close friends, a good spread of colleagues, the occasional hook-up, and an even less frequent girlfriend was good enough.

It also meant when Nate, her *best* friend, was unhappy with her, it rocked her world, and not in a good way. Nate was usually the one person she could count on to understand her. Hopefully he'd tell her how she could fix this, and then she'd...go do it. That worked most of the time. For an engineer, he usually had pretty good ideas.

"Willa says you barely talk to her, and you avoid her every chance you get. I know this is less than ideal, but come on."

What was she supposed to say? That, in truth, she liked Willa very much—too much—and she avoided her so she wouldn't say something stupid? Also so Willa wouldn't get wind of precisely how attractive Van found her? Confessing to Willa's doting older brother she had the hots for his baby sister wasn't something she was up for. Not this morning, and basically never. Especially because it wasn't like she was going to do anything about it. She'd never jeopardize her friendship with Nate for a few weeks with some girl. No matter how attractive that girl may be.

So instead of pleading her case or explaining herself as she usually did in the face of Nate's patience and understanding, she clammed up and offered only as much as she needed to get out of this conversation as soon as possible.

"I will attempt to be more personable."

"Good." Nate sounded gruffly satisfied, and she could picture him on the couch in his parents' living room in Fairfield, his cast-encased leg propped up on a pillow. His mom would probably bring him lemonade and popcorn, because that's how Mrs. Carter rolled. When she wasn't whipping her garden into shape or playing a game of doubles at their country club at any rate. "Now, are you on duty tonight, or can we do a live-tweet of *Serenity*? I'm bored as shit, and everyone I know is either working or off having fun without me."

"It's a hard-knock life," Van agreed as she clicked over to the tab of the browser to where her calendar was constantly open. "I've got nothing after dinner tonight. Eight o'clock?"

Nate sucked air through his teeth. "Ah, I'm not sure that's going to work for me. I have a very busy schedule of sitting on my ass and attempting to take a shower with a trash bag rubber-banded around my leg."

Later she'd send Nate a care package. By care package, she meant picking out a bunch of random awesome things off ThinkGeek and having them delivered to his doorstep. Because that's what friends were for. "Fine, we can make it eight-thirty. Talk to you then, Nathandridge Orville Carter."

———

WHEN WILLA GOT BACK from dinner, Van was at her desk as usual and typing furiously, which was not so usual. She also had her headphones on, and it looked like a split screen. It wasn't any of her business anyhow, so Willa went to the bathroom to get changed and then settled into her bed with one of her journals.

Occasionally her attention would be drawn across the room when Van would laugh, and her fingers were almost constantly flying over the keys. Was she talking to someone? If so, who? Willa felt a twinge of jealousy for whoever was able to engage Van so thoroughly. The most Willa had been able to get out of her were one-word answers, no matter how carefully she crafted the questions.

She was well aware she wasn't Nate, but surely she couldn't be that bad? Had she made a misstep somewhere, asking too many questions about Van's job? Or maybe that was it—Van didn't seem convinced Willa could hack it in academia. Which was a worry Willa had herself, and having a woman she respected and had had a crush on for…well, a long time, think she wasn't good enough either? Like maybe she should've stuck to her courts and balls and racquets? It hurt, more than Willa wanted it to and more than she'd admit. Which was why she'd been so vague when Nate had asked her how things were going with Van. Aside from saying not so great.

She'd barely confessed her fears about being out of her depth in her PhD program to Nate, and he'd done what he always did. Ruffled her hair and told her she'd be great. His enthusiasm and straightforward pep talks were usually all she needed to be ready to tackle her problems, but this felt different. Bigger, somehow, and something she didn't already have a rock-solid baseline confidence about. With time, it would get better. She'd keep slogging through her graduate program, and the longer she was there, the more proof she'd have she was meant to be. Until then, she'd have to brazen it out. In her PhD program and here at Camp Firefly Falls.

On the plus side, there were only four weeks left, and everything else was going great. Van laughed again, typed something with a flourish, and then slid her headphones off and closed her laptop. When she got up and turned around, there was a smile on her face, and she looked happy...until she saw Willa.

Van froze on the spot, and her face went blank. "Oh, hey. Didn't realize you were here. Sorry if I..."

Willa waved her concern away. "You were fine. I was reading before bed."

"Right. Well..." Van seemed poised to add something else, and Willa was waiting, waiting for it. *Talk to me. Tell me who had you sputtering with laughter and typing as fast as your fingers could move. Were you flirting? Was it a date?* Nate hadn't said anything about Van having a girlfriend or dating anyone, but why would he? It's not as though he would think Willa would want to be with Van— she'd always played her lust for Van close to her chest.

So maybe there was someone. Knowing Van, she was probably a freaking Nobel Prize winner or head of some fancy ass lab or something. The thought made envy spike in Willa's chest, and it didn't get any better as Van pointed toward the bathroom, muttered something, and ran a hand through her short-cropped hair before turning on her heel and heading into the bathroom. Great.

6

"I ASKED you both to come here because I need a favor."

Out of the corner of her eye, Willa noticed Van frown. Why was she so grouchy all the time? It was a good thing Willa was an optimist, because otherwise she would've started to take Van's behavior personally.

"Sure, Heather. What do you need?" Heather and Michael had rescued her from a depressing-as-all-hell summer in Stanford, so she'd be willing to do anything for them.

"With Tegan leaving early to get back to San Diego for her new job, I'm going to have to fill in as rec director too. There's not a whole lot of time for me to plan out and prepare for all the programming for the final session like I usually would. I've got a few ideas scribbled down for some of the activities, but I need some help coming up with the rest and you two have the lightest duties for the next several weeks. We've got Aquitaine Research and Consulting coming, and they've requested an eighties theme, which I am only too happy to provide. I mean, come on. *Pretty in Pink, The Breakfast Club, Dirty Dancing?*"

Yes. Even though Willa had entirely missed the eighties, she still had a nostalgia for it. Come to think of it, maybe that was why. All the best stuff had already been cherry-picked by the time she got to it, so she didn't have to suffer through the worst of it. Like shoulder pads, mullets, and super-high-cut leotards. *Shiver.*

"Neon, crimping your hair, stirrup pants, 'Thriller,' *Ferris Bueller's Day Off*? I am on it."

She and Heather high-fived each other and then turned to Van expectantly. Her arms were crossed over that crazy attractive vest of hers, and she looked at them over her round-rimmed glasses before making a tentative offer. "*Empire Strikes Back? Goonies? Ghostbusters?*"

Heather punched Van in the shoulder. "Yes! That's the spirit. See? I knew I could count on the two of you. This is going to be great."

Then Heather launched into instructions and hints, the things they would need, a rough budget. Meanwhile, all Willa could think was she'd be able to spend more time alongside Van. Maybe working with her on a project would let Van see she wasn't a kid anymore and was a competent adult, more than capable of taking on a career in academia. Even if she didn't, it would still be fun.

She'd always loved how Van's mind worked, because it didn't appear to operate the same way as anyone else's. Which was sometimes a problem—how could she find anything in her office, never mind in their cabin? But when it wasn't mystifying or frustrating, it was delightful. And useful. Exhibit A: the Wi-Fi in their cabin when the rest of the camp had none.

While Willa thought pretty squarely in the box—or in the court, as things may be—Van would look at the box, toss it over her shoulder, and declare she liked pyramids better. Because why the hell not? Then she'd solve the problem. Probably that's what had landed her that post-doc and her current tenure-track position.

Before Heather could get too carried away, Willa interrupted

"Can you write some of this stuff down and email it to us? I have to run to a lesson, and I'm sure Van's got some work to do."

Van shot her a grateful look, and pleasure nestled between Willa's ribs. She may not be Van's favorite person, but she at least knew enough about her to know leaving her alone with planning-mode Heather was a bad idea. Nate had sometimes had to run interference between Van and their parents. Willa had always known growing up that Van liked her family, but so much chattering and togetherness could throw her for a loop. Heather was more like the Carters than she was like Van, and leaving them in the same room to work on something so unstructured could go badly. Van would get overwhelmed and come off as rude, Heather would get frustrated, and this project she was so looking forward to would start off on the wrong foot.

Willa would make a good go-between for the two of them. Talking at Van was not a good way to communicate with her; the written word fared much better, and if you were going to talk, it helped to have your talking points organized. Heather was more of a dream-it-up-and-then-figure-it-out type.

Now that she'd done her good deed for the day, it was time to do her job.

———

VAN SCOWLED after Willa's retreating form. That damnably short skirt swirled around her thighs as she walked, her blonde hair bouncing in a too-perfect ponytail. Woman was like a goddamn shampoo commercial come to life.

But she couldn't stand around glowering; she needed to get out of there before Heather launched into more planning ideas. So she waved an awkward salute and mumbled something about having enough of the surveys from last session returned to start compiling the data and generating the report.

Downstairs in her office, she picked up her BB8 bouncy ball and threw it against the wall, catching it as it came back at her. She'd have to find a way to get through the next month of having to work so closely with a woman she found so maddeningly attractive, but whom she wouldn't touch. The activities planning would be a good distraction, even if the eighties weren't her strong suit. There was at least some good fodder for geeking out to.

Plus, she'd looked up Aquitaine, as she had all the other companies hosting weeks at Camp Firefly Falls, and they were actually pretty cool, as consulting firms went. They did predictive analytics and had a surprisingly female-heavy staff. If Van hadn't been so dead-set on academics since she'd first set foot on a college campus, Aquitaine would've been the type of place she could see herself working.

Innovative; germane to a much larger segment of the population than the miniscule number of people who studied the physics of protein folding; and, she would imagine, better paying. Plus, depending on the project, their employees probably got to work on more than one assignment at a time and in multiple industries. No fucking grant applications. Or, if there were, a support staff to write them for you.

No use dwelling on that. Aquitaine was coming to Firefly Falls for a corporate retreat, not to do job interviews, and even if they had been coming to recruit, Van had a job. The job she'd always wanted. The job she was going to have for the rest of her life.

That thought should have made her happy. Job security was awesome, and Willa had been right when she'd said tenure-track positions were becoming fewer and farther between. Van had busted her ass to get here and attaining that kind of life goal should've made her ecstatic. How many people could say they'd attained their biggest dream by the time they were thirty?

She caught BB-8 again as he bounced off the wall and looked in his camera. "Then why do I feel so bleak?"

It was her imagination, but she could practically hear the thing make a sad bloop. Yep, that was about right.

Van shook herself out of some of her melancholy and got back to work. She had social media posts to schedule, analytics to look at, and a newsletter template to revamp. She wanted to get all that done by lunch so she could deal with some of the nonsense from UVA before dinner. The UVA stuff she didn't want to do in her office because it would likely involve throwing things and swearing profusely.

It ended up taking her longer than expected, but by the time she and Heather had done their weekly check-in while chowing down on some of Meg's paella at lunch, she still felt pretty good. Good enough to head back to the cabin and face the bullshit. Willa would still be giving lessons, so she'd have the place to herself and could pitch fits to her heart's content. Except when she passed the tennis court, no one was there.

Maybe her last lesson had run late and she was still at lunch? It was possible. Or maybe she was helping someone else out with another activity? Willa was good about stuff like that. But no, when Van stepped into the cabin, there was Willa sitting on her bed, a coffee table book spread across her lap.

She looked up when she heard Van come in and smiled. It made Van want to smile back, but she couldn't quite make the shape with her face. "Hey. My lesson cancelled, so I came back here. I'll be out of your hair in an hour."

"You're not—" Really unfortunate visions of Willa's fingers running through her short-cropped hair made her close her eyes. "You're not in the way. You live here too."

Willa went back to flipping through the book on her lap, her hair in ridiculously adorable French braid pigtails today. There was no way Van was going to get started on stuff that would make her into a rage monster while Willa was here. If Nate had lectured her for ignoring Willa, she could only imagine what he would do if she scared his beloved baby sister. And actually, here was a chance to show she was not, in fact, ignoring Willa, because her efforts thus far had been less than stellar. Every time she even tried, she lost her nerve, because all she could see were the dominoes of her getting involved with Willa, her messing things up with Willa, and her inevitable demise when either Nate killed her or she lost his friendship and became so despondent she lost the will to live. But if this was what Nate wanted…

"What are you looking at?"

"Oh, this?" Willa closed the book but kept her page with a finger and turned it up so Van could see. It was a book about caverns of North America with a picture of a limestone cave on the front, a person standing in it for scale. The place was huge and pretty in a strange way. "My parents sent it to me when I declared my major. Because they're dorks like that."

Yes, the Carters were dorky, but in a sweet way. Van's parents had barely made it to her graduation. Van gestured to a spot next to Willa on the bed. "Mind if I sit?"

Willa's pale brows went up, but she said, "Sure," and patted the space right beside her. When Van sat down, Willa opened the book to the page she'd been looking at. It was a picture of some cave formations, and the caption said it was an image from Lehman Cave in Great Basin National Park.

"Have you been there?"

Willa traced the formation with her finger and got this dreamy look on her face. "Yeah, it's incredible. We went when I was in high school, and I think that was the first inkling I had that I liked geology. Well, technically, speleology, but whatever."

Van eyed the picture again, squinting and trying not to think about how sexy it had been when Willa said "speleology." *Unf.*

"You know, I can never remember which ones are stalactites and which ones are stalagmites."

"Neither can most people. The trick my mom taught me was stalagmites were on the ground, so you *might* trip over them."

"Yeah, but if they were on the ceiling, then they *might* fall on you."

Willa gave her a withering look, and she was almost sorry, but she couldn't help herself. "You're the worst."

Yeah, there was no way around that, so Van didn't even attempt to argue. "Basically."

"Another trick is stalagmites have a G, so they're on the ground, and stalactites have a C, so they're on the ceiling."

Given enough time, Van could probably figure out a way to ruin that mnemonic for Willa too, but she wouldn't. Not right now, anyway. Which was a wise decision, because completely unbidden, Willa started talking about rocks, more specifically speleothems. Showed Van pictures of cave popcorn, draperies, helictites, and soda straws. When she got to one particular picture, her eyes practically gleamed.

"These are shields. This is what my dissertation is on. We have a good idea of how most of the formations occur, but shields are still a mystery. Aren't they cool?"

Van had to concede yes, they were pretty cool, but the wonder that brightened Willa's face concerned her some. Partly because she recognized it from her own early days of grad school, and look where that had gotten her.

"Yeah, but you know if you become a professor, you're not going to spend all of your time climbing around in caves and taking cool pictures, right? That most of it is paperwork and annoying undergrads? There's lots of boring ass shit that has to be done that takes up way more time than the fun stuff."

Willa blinked at her, blue eyes wide, and then shrugged. "I

know, but there's crap that comes with every job. I still feel like this is better than most."

That was true, but academia had a certain mystique, a polish to it that drew people in with its shiny promises of tenure and the glamour of sabbaticals, the glory of having your name next to the next big discovery in your field. Once you got there, though, the gleam tended to wear off. She wanted Willa to make her choice with eyes wide open, not make the same mistake she had.

"Well, it's also worse in some ways, so think hard before you invest so many years of your life walking down that road. It's hard to turn back."

Willa opened her mouth to say something else, but then maybe thought better of it. "I've got to get ready for my next lesson, but I'll see you tonight? We've got a lot of work to do."

"Yep, see you tonight."

Van watched Willa gather up her things and tie on her sneakers. She wanted to grab Willa's blonde braids and force her to listen to a lecture on being careful about going into academia. It had made Van so unhappy, and that was the last thing she wanted to happen to Willa.

Willa's happiness mattered to her—and her dedication to geology surprised and delighted Van—and she wouldn't want to see the bounce that was in her step as she walked out the door to her lesson become a dull trudge toward university bureaucracy and politics. Much as she was trudging toward her laptop now.

7

AFTER THAT EVENING'S activities of wine and cheese tastings, combined with a paint night, followed by a stop at the nightly campfire, Willa made her way back to the cabin. She was going to have to find a way to push her feelings for Van to the back of her mind so she could focus on what was important: the job they had to do. Heather was pretty chill, but this camp was her life and she took the satisfaction of her guests very seriously.

Willa wasn't sure if she'd ever be able to come back here—it had been Nate's job after all and not hers—but she wanted Heather to *want* her to come back. She liked Heather and wanted the woman she respected so much for getting this business off the ground to think she was competent too. That meant rocking eighties week.

There were lights on in the cabin when Willa jogged up the stairs to their door, so Van was likely there. Before she entered, she gave a quick knock, and as she passed over the threshold, Van looked up at her from where she was lounging on her bed with her computer. She looked to be out of the funk she'd been in when Willa left earlier.

"How was drunk painting?"

"Awesome. We're going to have to work hard to make the last week as good as this one. I don't know how Heather does it because it's freaking amazing. If you have time right now, we could start brainstorming ideas for our week. It'll take us a while to organize our supplies and do the programming, so the sooner we get going, the better."

"Uh, sure. Let me send this email." Van frowned at her laptop screen, but her fingers didn't move on the keys.

"Is everything okay?" Not that Van was always some super-happy sunshiny person, but she tended to at least look…competent. Like she was in control of her world at any given moment. That ease was decidedly lacking at the moment.

"Yeah, it's…work stuff. Never mind, I'll deal with it later." She shut her laptop decisively and tossed it on the bed. "So what did you have in mind?"

"Well." Willa put her hands out, setting the scene for her pitch, and Van's brows shot up. Okay, she had Van's attention. "I thought before we get down to the nitty-gritty details, what we should do is immerse ourselves. You know, watch eighties movies, listen to eighties music. I'm not going to make you wear shoulder pads or put a scrunchie in your hair, but you get the idea."

"I do." Van's nose had wrinkled at the mention of scrunchies, but Willa couldn't blame her. Those had yet to come back in style, and there was a reason for it. Although when they did, she might still have quite the collection under her bed in Fairfield… *Focus, Carter.*

"I figure if we can distill our favorite things—and of course, Heather and some of the other staff can contribute ideas too— we'll have a pretty good shot at making this nostalgia come to life. What do you think?"

It was possible Van didn't look overly enthusiastic, but when she spoke, it was more positive than Willa had expected. "Sounds good, boss. Where do we start?"

———

Aw, crap. She was in trouble.

Van already knew Willa could dominate on the tennis court—enjoyed very much, actually, watching her do just that—and if the girl had gotten into grad school at Stanford, she had to be a damn good student, but now she was going to prove to be capable at event organizing too? That had never been one of Van's strong suits. Could she write papers? Yes. Put together a poster and a talk for colleagues? Absolutely. But those were her people. When it came to, well, *other* people, that was where she fumbled. There was a reason she hadn't been on prom committee or anything remotely like that in school.

For Willa to be so good at so many things...

Van knew, of course, other people found things like bodies and faces to be attractive. She did herself on occasion, particularly if it involved tan legs on a tennis court. But what really got her motor running was competence. It didn't even have to be in any specific area. Listening to people geek out about their favorite things was one of her great joys in life, and when someone was doing something they enjoyed *and* doing it well *and* happened to be the rare person who stirred Van's physical interest? That was competence porn wrapped up in a pretty package, and nothing made Van happier. Or hornier.

Willa was still on her feet, talking about her ideas, bouncing in her flip-flops as though she were on the tennis court and preparing for her opponent's serve. At least she had on some khaki shorts and not one of those sexy-as-hell skirts. Because when she wore those, all Van could think of was how easy it would be to put her palms to the outsides of Willa's knees, wrap her fingers around, and then slide up oh-so-slowly until she reached—

"So does that sound good? I thought we could start with *Footloose*, what do you say?"

Dammit. Apparently Willa didn't actually need to be wearing one of her skirts for Van's imagination to run wild. *Focus, Van. You didn't get your PhD in record time by getting distracted by girls.*

"Uh, sure. Yes. Absolutely." What was she even talking about? *Footloose* what? Was that the one with Kevin Bacon in it? If so, which Kevin Bacon one? Dude had been in freaking everything for a while.

"Cool. I'll grab the snacks."

At least there would be snacks.

Five minutes later, Willa was bounding onto Van's bed and sitting cross-legged beside her, offering a bag of what honest to god looked like dried seaweed. That wasn't food; that was fertilizer.

"No, thanks."

"Suit yourself. Okay, are we ready?"

Van had managed to gather the scattered remnants of her brain well enough to understand Willa expected her to conjure *Footloose* out of thin air. She cracked open her laptop again, minimizing the screen that had the nonsense from UVA on it. It was a good thing she had upped her data in order to make a hotspot, because the Wi-Fi around here was for shit, what with Heather and all her get-back-to-nature, focus-on-the-now stuff.

Luckily, one of the services she subscribed to had the movie streaming, and the signal should hold up well enough to watch it.

———

VAN DID NOT APPEAR to be entertained by the disembodied feet dancing on the screen in front of them. Which…how could you not be? They were hilarious. Also, Willa had always been sad she'd missed leg warmers. Could they come back in fashion so she could get in on that action?

As they watched, Willa became increasingly aware Van wasn't sitting in her normal preoccupied slouch. No, she was sitting there stiff as a board and wasn't appearing to enjoy this at all.

"Van?"

"Yeah?"

"Are you bored? Do you want to watch something else?"

"No. I...I liked the tractors," she offered absently, fingers curled into fists at the sides of her thighs. She was wearing a T-shirt that read *Safety Lights Are for Dudes*, and it was closer-fitting than her normal clothes. It, in fact, showed off a rather tantalizing outline of Van's small breasts.

"Well, you seem super-uncomfortable."

Even from her place at Van's side, Willa could see Van's dark eyes widen. Was she making Van uncomfortable?

"Do you want me to move? We could put your laptop on the desk, and I could sit—"

"No, it's fine. I'm just...cold."

That was an easy problem to fix. Willa hit pause on the screen and scooted off Van's bed to grab the blanket her parents had brought her from her old room. "Oh, I have a great idea. You remember how when we were little we would make movie forts with Nate? I bet we could rig one up here."

The blanket was barely big enough for the two of them plus the laptop—this used to be a lot easier when they were smaller. Eventually though, they had it set up so the two of them were huddled under a canopy of blanket and a glowing laptop.

She, Willa Carter, was snuggled under a blanket with Van. If Willa could direct the movie of her own life, this is definitely where Van would realize she was desperately in love with Willa, and they'd end up making out and maybe some, uh, other stuff.

As it was, she was enjoying immensely the feel of Van's body heat and the way she smelled right next to her. Close enough to—

God, Willa. Get your shit together. Van doesn't want you, and this wasn't for inappropriately hitting on her. You did this because she was cold. It was supposed to be considerate. So consider her. "Warmer now?"

Van didn't turn to face her, but instead stared at the screen where young Chris Penn was paused in the middle of suffering through his dance lessons.

"Yep."

Willa shook her head. What had happened to the Van she used to know? Yeah, it had been a long time, but she didn't remember her childhood hero/crush being quite so...monosyllabic. So she leaned forward and started up the movie again, trying to decide if this would be a good choice for one of their theme nights. Dancing was always good, but there were so many eighties dance movies—was this really the best one? Maybe she should've started with *Dirty Dancing*, but honestly Ren and his quirky clothes seemed more like Van's bag than Baby and Johnny Castle.

Whatever. There was only so much a girl could do, and she'd given it her best. For tonight.

———

How would Nate murder her? Maybe, more importantly, how would he dispose of her body? This was important for a few reasons. Foremost, because she was an organ donor, so if he could kill her in a way where it would still be possible to maintain the viability of her organs and tissues, that would be ideal. Also, she hoped he'd do it in a more central location, because if he disposed of her out here, the odds of her organs being usable by the time they got to a hospital where organ transplants were actually done were negligible.

And, dammit, Van didn't want her body parts to be wasted. They were perfectly good. For someone who spent most of her life looking at screens, anyhow. Maybe she'd send him a list of suggestions. It's not like she was going anywhere anytime soon, although her laptop was out of reach. Eh, her phone would do as well. She could sneak that out of her pocket and send him an email. She'd have to use her left hand to type, but again, it wasn't as though she was in a hurry. Truth be told, she would stay here indefinitely if it were up to her. Even though she was getting bored as hell with the start screen for *Footloose*.

Nate wasn't generally inclined to physical violence, but he'd probably make an exception for her. Either because she was having lustful thoughts that could lead to more than just thoughts, which could lead to Willa getting hurt, or because Nate would feel bad because he might feel like Van had "picked" Willa over him. Which wasn't true, at all. But she would rather Nate kill her than lose him.

Could Willa not have fallen asleep earlier in the movie? Then Van might've actually been able to enjoy it. Sure, it was a fine movie, and while she was nowhere near being a huge fan, she could understand the appeal. But what she would've liked more was Willa's head resting on her shoulder as they huddled under the blanket while the whole movie played.

As things were, she was caught in the awkward position of deciding how long to let Willa snooze peacefully while basically lying on her. If it were Nate, she'd punch him in the shoulder and be done with it. But Nate didn't smell this good—a combination of the citrusy shampoo Willa had a giant bottle of in their shower and the vaguely pine scent of spending all day out of doors around here—nor would his breath be misting softly across her collarbones. No, Nate would snore loudly and drool. They'd had enough sleepovers for her to know.

Now Van knew what it was like not just to sleep near Willa as she'd been doing for weeks, but to have Willa sleep *on* her. If Willa were her girlfriend, she would slide out from under her carefully, gently, and ease her onto the pillows and cover her with a blanket, hopefully not waking her up. If Willa did wake, it would be with a charming and sleepy smile. She'd grab onto the necktie Van was wearing and pull her down for a kiss. A soft kiss that might lead to more and…oh, god.

She had to wake Willa up. Had to. Because if she let the fantasy spool out, she'd never forget it. Also, she'd be soaking wet and her nipples would be hard, and that wasn't okay. If she waited too much longer, Willa would look at the time, realize it had been a pretty freaking long time since the movie had ended, and what had Van been doing since it had? Sitting there perving on her? Yes, but Willa didn't need to know that. Shit.

Van made a bargain with herself. It was a useful strategy, one she employed often. She could have five more minutes of Willa's blonde head on her shoulder, and then she'd wake her up. If asked why she hadn't done it sooner, well, not wanting to wake a person who was obviously tired was a good reason, wasn't it? Regular people would do that, right? Turned out she didn't have to.

A few seconds later, Willa stirred, nuzzled her face into Van's shoulder before she realized where she was and what she was doing, and whoo boy did Van enjoy the hell out of that. Out of her. All her fantasies went off like a supernova in her brain, and images of Willa kissing and licking her neck, cupping her cheek, and undressing her abounded. None of these things were okay, so she sat there stiff as carbyne, trying not to let little Willa Carter know what was going on in her head.

Soon, Willa sat up and was pushing the blanket off of them, stretching her arms up to the ceiling and yawning. "I am so sorry, Van. Must've been more tired than I thought from swimming this afternoon and the painting. Why didn't you wake me up?"

Because I very much enjoyed having physical contact with you? Because I liked how warm and heavy your head was resting on my shoulder? Because your breath on my collarbone was as good as a tropical breeze, and I would give up one of my best cosplay outfits to have had you kiss me there?

"You seemed tired. And it's not like you needed to see the movie again, so I let you sleep."

Willa smiled at her, and even though her hair was a disaster and one side of her face was pink and creased from where it had been resting on Van's shoulder, she looked beautiful. That was cool. It's not as if Van's heart got used much anyhow; it would function as well as she needed it to, stalled out or not. "Thanks, you're the best."

8

AFTER HER LAST lesson of the day, Willa showered in a rush, made a phone call, and then hopped in the Subaru, returning half an hour later with a giant, greasy cheese pizza. It was Van's night to pick a movie, which meant *Star Wars*, pizza, more *Star Wars*, snack food, more *Star Wars*, ice cream, and finally, more *Star Wars*.

Good thing they both had the day off tomorrow because Willa was going to need it—both to sleep in after such a marathon session and possibly run an actual marathon after that much food.

Other than being concerned for her health, though, she was in a fantastic mood as she climbed out of the car with the finest pizza to be found in Briarsted—which wasn't saying much. Still.

She jogged up the steps to their cabin, and when she opened the door, she was bowled over by what was inside. It was dark, but stars spun on the ceiling, projected from a gadget on the floor; there were cardboard cutout figures of half a dozen characters she recognized from the movies; not to mention she almost walked into some sort of spacecraft that appeared to be suspended in midair. Was it a TIE fighter or an X-wing? She always got them confused. That and R2-D2 and C-3PO. She would not be mentioning that to Van, though, no sir.

Van climbed down from her bed, which she appeared to have been standing on in order to attach an inflatable Death Star to the corner. "What do you think?"

"I think..." *You're such a geek and I love you for it? I could listen to you talk about* Star Wars *for the rest of my life and tease me when I can't tell the difference between a Wookie and an Ewok?* "I think...you must have been keeping Amazon super-busy delivering all this stuff. How did I not notice all the boxes?"

Even in the darkened room, Van managed to look sheepish. "I didn't have to order any of this."

Willa looked around at all the memorabilia on display, seeing even more things than she had before, like a BB-8 pillow and the fact Van was wearing...

"Are you supposed to be Han Solo?"

A broad grin spread across Van's face. "I wasn't sure you'd notice. How could you tell?"

It was true if she'd dressed up as one of the more obscure characters, Willa never would've gotten it, but with the fitted black pants, the cream shirt with the open neckline, the black vest slung over it, and a utility belt wrapped around her hips, it was unmistakable. Plus, even as a kid she'd had a crush on Harrison Ford and things hadn't changed all that much. Damn did Van look fine.

"I may not be a *Star Wars* aficionado like you, but I remember Han Solo. Do I get a costume too?"

She meant it as a joke, but Van's gaze slid from hers over to her bed. On top of her duvet, there was a white...something.

"Oh my god, I get to be Princess Leia?"

"Only if you want, I wasn't sure if you'd—"

Willa crossed the room in three long strides and grabbed ahold of Van, pulling her into a full-contact hug. "I want. This is awesome. I'm so excited about it. Did you have this just lying around too?" Releasing Van, who'd gone stiff as a board in her arms, Willa took a step back. "Sorry, I didn't mean to...well, sorry."

"Don't be sorry. It's not that I don't like hugs, it just takes me a while to get used to them. I don't...touch people much. Not like you and Nate and your parents. I guess I'm out of practice. To answer your question, though, no, I didn't have that before. That I had to order."

Willa's heart melted into a puddle. Van had gotten her a costume? She wanted to share this with Willa—and not only share it by decorating their cabin, but include her? She stepped forward again, settling the toes of her sneakers in between the tips of Van's black boots.

"I'm going to hug you now. Just FYI. You can tell me not to and I won't, but I'd like to. And I'll try to give you time to get used to it, okay?"

Van bit her bottom lip and released it on a sigh, as though she was preparing to go into some epic battle. "Okay. I'm ready."

So Willa put her arms around Van again and held her, their chests pressing against each other. After a second, Van's arms reached tentatively around Willa's waist, her hand eventually coming to rest between Willa's shoulder blades. Hell if that didn't feel good. She could almost imagine pulling apart enough to press her mouth to Van's, to run her tongue along where Van's teeth had sunk into her bottom lip, but she didn't want to freak her out. Plus, she wanted to wear her outfit.

Willa counted to a hundred twenty, enjoying the gradual softening of Van's body against her, as well as the feel of Van's breath against her shoulder and the smell of her. Slightly musty because god knew where she'd been keeping her secret stash of *Star Wars* clothes, but also warm and smelling like the ocean. A warm salty body Willa wanted to lick. Instead, she let go of Van and stepped back, regretting it the second their bodies were no longer pressed together.

It was possible Van's cheeks were pink, but it was hard to tell in the low light. Willa wasn't so sure she wasn't sporting a flush herself.

"Uh, I guess I should get dressed?"

"Yeah, I'll get stuff set up."

Van turned away from Willa, and she couldn't help but admire how the black pants hugged Van's hips, her butt. Han Solo was a good look for her. Willa grabbed the pile of white fabric from off her own bed and toted it into the bathroom, shutting the door and trying not to swoon like a schoolgirl after she'd closed it. But why the hell not? It's not as though Van could see her if she did. So full-on schoolgirl, hand-on-forehead, back-against-the-door, little-squeal swoon it was.

———

WHILE WILLA WAS in the bathroom, getting naked to change into the Princess Leia dress Van had ordered for her, Van distracted herself by cracking the pizza open and digging in. Meg did a great job with the food, especially considering she had to cook for so many people and deal with a different set of dietary restrictions every week, but pizza was not her specialty. Or maybe it was and Van couldn't appreciate it. Too fancy for her taste—Meg was always trying to put figs or some shit on it. Cheese. That was what was supposed to be on pizza. Maybe pepperoni, but not figs for god's sake.

Van was about halfway through her slice when the bathroom door opened, and Willa stepped out, a vision in white. It made Van wish she'd gone for the slave girl bikini set...almost. Truthfully, while she'd love to see Willa's muscular arms and taut stomach, the thing that killed her most was the look of raw delight on Willa's face.

"Do I look okay?"

"Yeah." Van had to clear her throat and refrain from stuffing the rest of her slice into her mouth to keep her from saying something far too honest. *Keep it simple, stupid.* "You look great."

Willa twirled, and Van's heart exploded like the Death Star. Why did she love making Willa happy so goddamn much? But she did. Made her feel like Emperor of the entire galaxy, except not in an evil way. Well, not super-evil, though she definitely wanted to do some naughty things to Willa.

"Except my hair. It's all wrong." Willa picked up a honey lock and looked at it disapprovingly. "Even I know Leia is not blonde, and there's no way I can do those fancy cinnamon roll things she's got on the sides of her head."

"I could help you with that if you want. After we finish the pizza. Don't want to get your hair all…" Van held up her hand, fingers slick with grease.

"Can you really?"

"Uh, yeah."

"You don't seem like a hair expert. No offense."

Right. Her own close-cropped 'do wouldn't inspire confidence. "Well, not on myself, but when I go to a comic con or something, it's nice to be able to help the people I'm cosplaying with. So I picked up a trick or two."

She shrugged, hoping against hope Willa wouldn't see how much Van wanted to sink her fingers into Willa's hair, twist and pin it into Leia's trademark buns. Who cared if Willa was blonde? It was the spirit that mattered, right? Willa had the perfect mix of badass and beauty that Leia did. Also that regal bearing. Yep.

"That's awesome. And yes, after pizza, because I'm starving."

Then Willa was standing next to her, reaching into the box and pulling out a slice and bringing it to her mouth. Van couldn't stop staring. When Willa looked at her after taking a bite, Van tore her gaze away so her cabinmate wouldn't be able to tell all the filthy ideas shooting through her head like hits from a blaster. Fuck, she was in trouble.

To cover up her unacceptable feelings toward Willa, Van set up the movie and got everything settled, putting the pizza box in between them on a beach towel on her bed. Good. The threat of getting cheese and tomato sauce on her vintage *Star Wars* comforter should be enough to stop her from accosting Willa, whose eyes were focused on the screen as if she hadn't watched the opening credits to *Star Wars* well over a hundred times. Or maybe that was Van.

They decimated the pizza in pretty short order, and while Van wouldn't have mentioned it again, Willa wiped her fingers thoroughly on some napkins and reached forward to pause the movie on Van's laptop before turning to her. "Pizza's gone. Can you do my hair now?"

Can I thread my fingers through your silky blonde hair, let it fall over your sculpted shoulders, and smell it at every opportunity while I make you look like one of film history's most iconic heroines? "Uh, sure. Lemme wash up."

Paper napkins were well and good for most intents and purposes, but she wouldn't chance Willa's hair to such a careless measure.

When she emerged from the bathroom, hands squeaky clean and practically twitching with the need to touch Willa, she found Willa had set up the laptop on a stack of books on the carpet and positioned herself on the floor before it, leaning up against Van's bed. And where the pizza box had been were now a brush, a comb, some elastics, and bobby pins. Willa had come prepared.

Despite her heart beating hard against her ribs, Van ambled over as if she had all the time in the world and only passing interest in what they were doing, when in fact this would probably be the most achingly pleasurable thing she'd done in months, if not years. So painful with unrequited desire, but so goddamn delightful with the mere ability to touch the woman she'd been thirsting for.

So she climbed up behind Willa, settling her knees alongside Willa's shoulders and trying not to imagine what it would be like for Willa to turn around, push her to her back, and yank her pants off, the hunger in her voice unmistakable as she'd say, "I want you."

Wow, did sex ever make people stupid. No time for her own private *Star Wars*-themed porno running through her head. Nope, not even a little bit. She was supposed to be putting years of cosplaying hairstyling to good use for her bunkmate who was indulging her.

Willa started the movie again, and when she leaned back, Van took up the brush and began to work it through Willa's hair. Soft, yes, and smelling of that citrus shampoo she'd like to huff like a middle schooler with a handful of Sharpies.

Willa's powerful shoulders dropped, and she let out a sigh of what could only be pleasure and tipped her head to give Van easier access to the side she was running the bristles through. It wasn't hard, not too many knots to be untangled despite its length, but given Willa's reaction, Van wanted to find an excuse to keep doing this for…forever.

Breathing dreamy sighs and settling until her head was resting on Van's knee, Willa was clearly enjoying herself. Maybe more than Van, and that was saying something given the pleasantly warm tingle that had set up shop in Van's chest with satellite locations all along her nervous system. Who knew brushing someone's hair could be so enchanting?

At some point, Willa's small sounds became kitten-sleepy, and Van nudged her with a knee. "Don't fall asleep or we'll have to start all over."

"I'm not asleep, just...blissed out. It's nice to have someone play with your hair, you know? It's not something that happens often after slumber party days are over. I mean, sure, sometimes people you're sleeping with will give you the odd pat on the head, but I can't tell you how long it's been since someone brushed my hair. It's nice. Like scalp-massage-at-the-salon nice."

Right. Slumber parties. A hair salon. Willa was carefully aligning this with other indulgent but strictly platonic experiences and some of Van's pleasure dimmed. Well, sure. What had she expected? For Willa to suddenly be enamored of her for brushing her hair? *For such a smart person, you can be awfully stupid sometimes.*

As an act of self-care, a way to guard her heart against further incursion from this clueless woman she had trapped between her legs, Van dropped the brush and picked up the comb. And as she had with so many friends before, cupped Willa's jaw and tilted her head back. "Chin up."

That was how you could see their hairlines, to make a straight part. She'd done it probably dozens of times, and never before had she wanted to keep tipping, far enough to lay a kiss on Willa's parted lips. Particularly when Willa blinked at her, dazed, and smiled. "Yes, ma'am."

Van had to close her eyes for a second before she could bring herself to locate the center of Willa's forehead, at the point of the tiniest widow's peak, and then she was running the comb through, about halfway back, until she could use it to flip Willa's hair to the sides. It was a relief to not have to look at her face, but to focus on the back of her head, and then to tip it down to finish making the division along her scalp. All the way until the comb reached to the nape of her neck and then it was a struggle again not to lean down and tease Willa with a brush of her nose and then her lips to the bared skin.

Focus, Thompson. Van made a mental note never to cosplay

with Willa again. At least not in anything that would require her assistance. This was torture. Brutal torture. Aiming to get this over with, Van made a tight ponytail over Willa's ear and then started to twist her blonde hair into a coil which soon started to twist in on itself. Van followed its lead, wrapping it in layers until a perfectly swirled cinnamon bun had shaped itself over Willa's ear. Not quite as voluminous as Leia's, but who had hair like that for real?

Carefully, she inserted pins, doing her best to secure the style without digging the metal into Willa's scalp, because ouch. Not that she had a ton of experience with bobby pins in her own hair —because honestly, what would she need them for?—but she'd heard her sisters shriek in protest during their ballet days when their mother was trying to get their hair into the perfect ballerina bun. It had sounded like cats being murdered.

For all it looked as though it should take hours, the twisty buns were relatively quick to accomplish once you'd had some practice, and Van had had plenty. It was a matter of only about ten minutes before—both thankfully and regretfully—Van was pushing the final pin in.

Once she was finished, she took one bun in each hand and bopped Willa's head back and forth, from one shoulder to another, and Willa laughed. "I don't remember Han Solo doing that to Leia in the movies."

"Yeah, but I bet he wanted to. Super-bad." Lucky bastard had gotten to kiss—and more—his Leia at some point. "Usually I'd use some transparent nets and a shit ton of hairspray to keep it this way, but since we're hanging out and not trying to push our way through the hordes at a convention, I figure you're fine without. So, you know, all done."

She patted Willa on the shoulder awkwardly because if she touched her more than that, she wasn't sure she'd be able to stop.

Willa reached forward and paused the movie once more before springing to her feet and spinning around.

"How do I look?"

Hell. Perfect. She looked perfect, but Van managed to choke out only a "fine," before Willa was jogging to the bathroom—did the woman ever *walk* anywhere?

"Dude, I don't know what you're talking about. I look amazing."

Yeah, you do.

Willa poked her head out again. "Seriously, I look awesome. I know my coloring is all wrong—" *No way, you're perfect exactly how you are* "—but aside from that, I look fan-freaking-tastic. For realsies. This is fun. We're definitely going to have to do a *Star Wars* event during the week. I know the first movie technically came out during the seventies, but still."

Van let Willa chatter excitedly about all the fun things they could do—make your own light sabers, a Death Star piñata, clearly a costume dinner—and tried not to be too depressed. Because surely some hunk of man-meat filling out a Han costume better than she could or maybe some lithe woman dressed up as Rey would hit on Willa, and she'd have to watch her flirt with someone else. If Willa were anyone else but Nate's little sister…but she wasn't.

It hurt too much, and she couldn't bear it. "Can we start the movie again?"

Willa's excited expression and buzzing ideas all collapsed. "Yeah, sure."

She climbed back up next to Van and pressed play, and they went back to watching the movie.

9

WHY DID Van always have to be such a fucking buzzkill? She didn't remember her being that way when they were kids. If anything, Van was the one who had never tired, who had urged Nate to make one more rocket, to watch one more movie, to play one more video game. She'd been like a geeked out Energizer Bunny on Red Bull. And now...

Willa had never worried all that much if people liked her. Truthfully, because most people did. She was easy to get along with, smart but not what some people would feel was annoyingly so, pretty but not in a way that usually inspired jealousy, and she did her best to be nice to people. Above all, she had no reason to think people *wouldn't* like her.

But Van was shooting holes in that theory all over the damn place. She'd tried to be a considerate cabinmate and not drive Van too crazy, but for whatever reason, she hadn't succeeded. At least not enough. Van ran hot and cold on her constantly, and she was starting to be tweaked by it. It wasn't fair.

They'd watched two of the movies and were about to start on the third. Van was off grabbing her idea of snack food—apparently kale chips didn't count—and Willa decided she'd had enough.

Van came back and tossed a bag of Bugles into Willa's lap—which, to be fair, were secretly one of her favorite junk foods, but where did one find Bugles outside of a gas station or an airport? —and stood in front of Willa with a carton of Double Stuf Oreos in her hands.

"Ready?"

"No. I have a question."

Van nodded as she ripped open the side of the carton, even though it specifically said *Open Here* at a flap on the top. "You've come to the right place. I was MIT's *Star Wars* trivia winner four years in a row. Shoot."

"Do you hate me?"

Van froze with one of the cookies halfway to her mouth. "Hate you? Why would you think that?"

"Sometimes you're nice to me, but then you act all weird, like maybe being nice was too taxing and you're done with it, have to rest up until the next time you can find the energy to talk and joke with me. Did Nate threaten you? Because I have to say, if you can't stand me, I'd rather we be colleagues and get our shit done and not pretend we're…" *Friends, moron, say friends, because she's not going to like you any better if she knows you've had a major crush on her for basically forever.* "…friends or whatever."

A small crease formed between Van's brows and her mouth crunched to the side. "I don't hate you."

"Well then, why—"

Van looked toward the ceiling where a model of the Millennium Falcon was dangling from a beam and blew an impatient breath through her nose. "I don't hate you, okay? Can we leave it at that?"

"No, we can't. I won't tell Nate if you don't want to keep up this façade. He won't know you still think of me as an annoying tagalong you put up with."

"That is not how I think of you at all. You're not annoying, you're not a tagalong, and I don't put up with you. I—"

She seemed to choke on whatever she was going to say next and set the Oreos on her desk in order to run both hands through her hair, making it stand on end instead of being floppy like Han's.

"What, Van? Tell me. Because I don't get it. I'm sorry your summer with Nate got ruined, okay? But it wasn't my fault."

"I know. You saved Nate's ass, along with the Tullys' which is awesome. Everyone who takes lessons with you raves about you, and you're doing a great job planning for this eighties week. Really, I don't hate you. Altogether, I think you're..." Van's lips flattened into a reluctant line. "I like you, okay? And not I-don't-hate-you levels of like, but Nate-would-probably-kill-me levels of like."

What? Willa sat there, feeling concussed. As though she'd stood in front of a ball machine turned on high and hadn't moved out of the way when the ball spit out and now her brain was knocking around in her skull. "You like me? As in, *like* me like me?"

Some words, many of which Willa would've wagered were swear words, made their way out of Van's mouth, under her breath. "Yes, okay? I *like* you like you. You're beautiful and strong and smarter than I ever gave you credit for. You work hard, I've loved hanging out with you, and you look phenomenal in your tennis whites. What exactly is there not to like? Are you happy now?"

Whoa. The buzzing in her ears, the full-body flush, the feeling like she was going to fall over even though she was sitting down. Those things weren't normal. Maybe she was asleep? She'd fallen asleep during their movie marathon before and maybe that could explain it, but she pinched her wrist and didn't wake up. So, okay, not a dream. Which meant there was only one thing to do.

Willa climbed off her perch on the bed, setting the Bugles to the side, because what she was about to do would require empty hands unburdened by horn-shaped corn snacks. Emboldened by Van's exasperated confession, she strode up to her for the third time that night, impinging on her personal space to the extent Van had to look up slightly into her face.

"The feeling is mutual." Then Willa kissed her, taking Van's round face between her hands so Van couldn't slip away.

Being forewarned about her initial reaction to physical contact, Willa didn't panic when Van went rigid, but held on, sustaining a gentle pressure, not bidding for anything more, even though she ached to part Van's lips with her tongue and explore her mouth. *Patience, Willa, have patience.*

Her persistence was rewarded by hands landing on her waist and a responding press of Van's mouth against her own and, soon enough, a shy insinuation of Van's tongue against the seam of her lips. *Yes.*

Willa welcomed the incursion with a slight spread and a dart of her own tongue to touch Van's, beating a quick retreat because she didn't want to overwhelm Van. Van who she was kissing, Van who'd confessed to liking her, Van whose hands were climbing steadily up her back, clinging to her like she never wanted to let go.

They kissed for a minute before Van pulled away, and though Willa was reluctant to let her go, she'd move at the speed Van was able to go. If that meant stopping, then she'd stop.

"How important is it that we finish this movie tonight?"

"Um…" Really? Van wanted to talk about *The Return of the Jedi* right now? If that's what Van needed, then she'd do it, but *come on.*

"Because I'd rather make out with you than watch it, but if it's important, I could probably... No, I can't hold off. I've been wanting to do that since you climbed out of your parents' station wagon. Here's a summary: Slave Leia, Yoda dies, Ewoks, Darth Vader dies, and then...then, this."

Van's fingers worked their way under the buns she herself had wound up only a few hours ago and pulled Willa into her, kissing her quite thoroughly. Damn. Not that it was a surprise, exactly, because Van was a passionate person, but never had she seen Van be passionate about a *person*; only science, fandoms, and feats of engineering. Feeling like she was up there in Van's estimation was far more satisfying than it ought to be, especially when Van slipped her tongue fully into Willa's mouth, not shy anymore, and caressed Willa's tongue with her own, drawing a groan out of Willa.

Arms around each other, they fumbled for the bed, pushing the snacks out of the way and trying to find a comfortable way to lie on the twin bed together, finally settling with Van on top, their bodies tangling until Willa wrapped a leg around Van's waist and pulled her down because she wanted more.

More of Van's mouth, more of the breathy satisfied moans Van was making, more of Van's hands roaming possessively over her. More of Van's hips pushing against her own and making her core pulse with want. Their breasts pressed together, and Willa wanted to strip Van out of her shirt, see the body she'd wondered about almost as much as she'd wondered about what it must be like to have Van's mind.

Hoping she wouldn't scare Van off by asking for too much, too soon, she separated from those lips and said a prayer before getting on with it. "I'd like to take this off you," she said, tugging at the black vest and then the cream, deep-necked shirt. "And this."

There was a split-second pause, and Willa braced herself for disappointment. Van had mentioned something about Nate killing her. Was that going to stop her from doing what they both clearly wanted? She hoped not, but she couldn't—

"Please." The word was barely out of Van's mouth before they were both reaching to peel the clothing away.

Willa managed the vest while Van tugged the shirt from her waistband, tossing the thing to the floor, and there she was, looming above Willa, utility belt still on, which for some reason Willa found kinda hot. What was even more mouth-watering was Van's bare skin.

Soft abdomen; small, high breasts with dark brown nipples that had already drawn into hard points; no freckles like Willa had all over. Willa didn't hesitate to reach up and cup Van's breasts in her hands, run her thumbs over the peaks of Van's nipples, and god did she love it when Van squirmed over her.

"I'm really—ah—sensitive. That feels—"

"Too much?" Willa asked, strumming her thumbs across the hard buds again and then circling them, careful not to touch.

"No, not too much. Just know you're going to—ngh—make me frigging crazy doing that." Van's eyes were squeezed tightly shut, and she rocked her hips against Willa.

What kind of woman would Willa be if she didn't take that as more of a promise than a threat? Was there something she wanted more in this moment than to drive Van up a goddamn wall? No. No, there was not.

While it was fun to handle Van, what Willa wanted more than anything was to make that woman lose that focused, steady mind of hers. She wanted to take her out of her brain for once and put her firmly in her body, which was being lovingly tormented. No better way to do that than with her mouth.

Willa wrapped her arms around Van's back and, with one hand firmly between her shoulder blades and another at her lower back, pulled her down until Van's breasts were level with Willa's open mouth.

"Willa, please, I—"

It's possible a protest would've followed, except it ended up languishing in Van's mouth while Willa worked first one of Van's nipples with her tongue and teeth and then the other. Which had the magical effect of shutting Van the hell up—or at least making her incoherent. Those sounds were a balm to Willa's ears. That she could reduce the smartest person she knew to nonsensical babbling, pleading, or even feral noises because she was so taken by what Willa was doing.

A nice ego boost too, for the part of Willa that wasn't entirely confident in her ability to please women in bed. She'd always liked girls, found them attractive, wanted to be with them, but it had taken her until her senior year in college to get up the nerve to do more than kiss one drunkenly at a party. Now here she was, sexing up her first crush—mind...blown.

She stopped long enough to catch her breath and let Van maybe find some words. She'd love to get Van off, but if there was one thing she'd learned from her last few girlfriends, it was that women were far more complicated than men. Making a woman come took finesse, attention, time. She wanted to learn what Van liked and then do it. Do all the things and make her head explode.

"Want to see you. Touch you."

Oh, she'd scored incomplete sentences, excellent. Then she remembered she wasn't wearing anything approaching normal for her—no, she had on this white...thing and it was going to have to come off. Like, all the way off. Because if Van wanted to touch her, she wasn't going to argue.

Getting out from under Van was a less-than-graceful operation, given how entangled they'd become, but she finally managed to stand up to the side of the bed and loved the look in Van's eyes as she rucked the skirt up to pull the long white dress over her head. Practically drooling, her Han was.

Willa managed to tear her eyes off the topless woman in front of her long enough to draw the Leia costume over her head, and then she was standing there in nothing but a bra and underwear. Not even a sexy bra and definitely not sexy underwear. But for the way Van's gaze was raking her body, they may as well have come from La Perla instead of Target.

If the heat pouring off Van was literal instead of metaphorical, Willa would have been quite comfortable standing there in her skivvies, but as things were, it wasn't warm in the cabin and gooseflesh started to pebble all over her body. Nothing said "fuck me" like goosebumps.

Lucky for her, Van noticed almost immediately and, after mumbling some apologies, threw her BB-8 pillow on the floor and drew back her comforter to invite Willa under her sheets. The idea of snuggling with Van in a bunk with the potential for oh so much more made Willa's knees wobble and she was only too glad to climb in alongside Van.

Once they were lying side by side, Van's hand landed on her waist. "You…you look even better naked than I ever imagined. I thank the tennis gods every day that you love to play because it's given you a phenomenal ass and legs and…well, everything. Over the past few weeks, I've imagined you getting naked more than I'd like to admit."

Heat bloomed on Willa's cheeks. "You have?"

"Uh, yeah. I don't actually usually take such long showers."

Oh. My. God. Then why had Van been avoiding her? She could try to figure that out, or she could get it on with the most incredible woman she knew. At the moment? No contest.

"Then will you show me? What you were doing? If you weren't just standing under the water anyhow."

Van's dark eyes glinted back at her, and a smile made her mouth curl up at one corner. "Want to help?"

"Uh, yes, yes, I do."

Before they could get there, there was more kissing. Van took off that sexy-as-fuck utility belt but didn't seem in any hurry to disrobe further. When Willa didn't think she could take it anymore, she reached for Van's fly and undid the button before sliding down the zipper, hardly believing what she was about to do.

Once the fly was down, she and Van worked in tandem to wriggle the fitted pants down her legs, and then they were only in their underwear.

Willa gestured to the grey boycut shorts with the Wonder Woman logo on the front. Wonder Woman was right; holy hell did Van look amazing, her hips flaring out from her waist. "Would it be presumptuous to take these off too?"

"No, not at all." This time Willa took matters into her own hands and urged Van's hips up as she peeled the cotton down Van's legs. And then... Van. Naked. It was strange in a way—she'd seen Van in a bathing suit countless times, but somehow her body seemed different here and now. Laid out like a buffet for Willa to take what she would, and she wanted it all.

They kissed more and pressed their bodies together underneath the sheets before Willa threaded her fingers through Van's. "Is it show-and-tell time yet?"

"Show-and-tell?"

"Yeah." She let a saucy smile spread across her face. "You show me what to do and then tell me how it feels."

Van's eyes widened, and it was possible her pupils dilated, though it was hard to say for certain in this low light. The arousal came through loud and clear in her breathy voice, though. "Best version of show-and-tell ever."

They shifted so Van was on her back, Willa curling into her side and using a hand to pry Van's knees open before dragging her fingertips up Van's inner thigh toward the promised land. As soon as she reached pubic hair, Van bit her lip in an effort to stifle a groan and then took Willa by the wrist. Laying her short, blunt fingers over Willa's, she slid their hands in tandem until their middle fingers parted Van's labia, and *there*.

Even if Willa didn't recognize the particular feel, she would've known they'd grazed Van's clit by the way Van sucked air through her teeth and pressed her head back into the pillow. Then she was urging Willa's finger into tight circles around the little bud, harder and faster than Willa touched herself.

The way Van's hips rocked up to meet their touch was a delight, as was her breath coming hard and close, the inhales and exhales clipped with effort and arousal. Willa wasn't sure what to expect—she'd never much enjoyed it when people had tried to make her come this way, but Van seemed well on her way.

Willa lowered her head, kissed Van's neck up to her ear, and whispered. "Do you need anything else?"

Van tossed her head on the pillow—*no, no*—and instead used Willa's hand gripped in hers to speed the circles further. The way Willa's finger slicked over Van's most intimate parts made her want to devour the woman who was coming apart at her touch. Maybe someday she'd get to taste Van—the idea made her squirm, rocking her own hips against Van whose cheeks had flushed. Movements still purposeful and rhythmic, Willa couldn't wait until she lost it. With a few more revolutions around Van's clit, she did.

A small choked cry and a few last uneven bucks of her hips, Van kept their entwined fingers pressed to her core as she shuddered with pleasure.

"Wills. Dammit, Wills."

Willa didn't want to hear Van anymore, she wanted to taste her, so she leaned down to kiss her and managed to wring a few more beats of climax from the body collapsed beneath her. Was this what Van had done, leaning up against the white subway tiles that lined the shower? Because heaven above was that hot as fuck.

When the urgency had abated—at least for Van, Willa's body was still strung taut with wanting—they kissed languidly, their mouths moving affectionately with each other, small nips and tinier licks until they came few and far between and Willa was resting her head on Van's shoulder.

They breathed together for a while, Willa still buzzing with desire, but also strangely content. This was not at all how she'd foreseen the night going, but this was way better than anything she could've imagined. She stroked Van's arm and enjoyed the smell of her skin. She smelled like, like…water.

Which was a strange thing to say, because water didn't smell. She supposed it was how things were grape-flavored—they didn't actually taste a lick like grape, but everyone knew what you meant if you said that. So, yeah, Van smelled like water. Cool and clean with a salty tang.

It was close enough Willa could practically hear the ocean waves rolling in and did that ever make her tired. But Van apparently had ideas other than sleep.

Her hand, small and warm, nudged at Willa's hip to roll her over onto her back and then caressed her side, from ribcage to hip and back again. A firm, comforting touch that sent Willa further into the dreamy space she'd been headed toward. Unhurried and languorous, she was content to let Van touch her however she wanted to.

It wasn't so long before the contact became less soothing and more sensual and then downright erotic, Van cupping Willa's breasts over her bra and thumbing her nipples through the fabric. Hands squeezed, fingers pinched, and Willa inhaled audibly. Van never took Willa's bra off or pushed the cups down, but the tiny distance was delicious in its own way—when Van finally touched her, the trigger she'd cocked would go off.

Then Van smoothed her hand down Willa's stomach until the heel met Willa's pubic bone and Willa rocked her hips to meet it, the pressure sending a bolt of electricity straight to Willa's clit.

"Please, Van."

Van kissed her, and while it was amazing—the taste and texture of her, the heat of her breath still new and surprising—it wasn't what she wanted.

"Your fingers, your hands, I want more. Will you make me come? Please?"

"Think I can?" Van's teasing murmur was soft as she stared down to where her hand was pressed against Willa. Applying more pressure, she blinked her dark eyes up to Willa's, and Willa's breath caught before she could even answer. From the smug look on her face, Van damn well knew she could do it, but she wanted Willa to say it. The woman was going to drive her crazy and was Willa ever going to enjoy the ride.

"Yes, yes, I think you can. Please, I want you inside of me."

Van nodded as if she were taking Willa's words under advisement, but she would do whatever she damn well pleased. Knowing Van, she probably would, but there would be no way Willa would regret it. Then Van was leaning over her, taking Willa's bottom lip between her teeth and sucking. Why was it Van knew how to make crackles of desire buzz through her erotic nerve system?

Van released Willa's lip, only to dip her tongue into Willa's mouth, and at the same time slip her hand into Willa's underwear, fingers coasting temptingly over Willa's clit and then farther back to where Willa was, dear god, so wet. Even before Van said it, she knew.

"Jesus, Wills, you feel so good. So wet for me." Then she was slicking the moisture back up to Willa's clit where she circled and rubbed, toyed with her.

"Please," Willa begged. This was nice, the fingers dancing over her sensitive flesh, but what she wanted, what her body ached for, was—

Van's fingers drove back, and then two of them were inside her.

"Yes."

It came out a desperate hiss, and Willa laid a hand over Van's, urging her to press her fingers farther, possess Willa more, reach that perfect place inside that would make her eyes cross. Van wasn't in a hurry. She kept a rhythm that was tempting, not satisfying, and wouldn't fuck Willa as hard as she wanted with her impossibly clever fingers.

"More. More!"

"Your manners are atrocious, you know that?"

Willa had gone from languid and dreamy to flat-out desperate, and she wasn't even sorry. "My manners? What about yours? You could make me come, and you won't."

"Fine." God was that confidence of hers sexy, that know-it-all attitude and the cocky way she smiled down at Willa. "But someday, I'm going to make you wait. I'm going to torture you until you're a writhing mess, and then I'm going to give you the orgasm of your life with my head between your legs."

Fuck it all. With a change in angle of Van's clever fingers, a few hard thrusts of her hand and the image of Van putting her mouth to work at the juncture of Willa's thighs, Willa gave in. Her internal muscles clenched around Van's fingers, and she rocked her hips so her clit could get that delicious contact with the heel of Van's hand, and oh that was heavenly. Made her feel as though she was zooming up through the clouds and passing angels on her way toward the heat and the light of the sun.

Her cry wasn't as muffled as Van's had been and she had a split-second of wondering if the next cabin over would be able to hear her shouts of ecstasy, but who the fuck cared? Another wave hit her, and she drowned in it, closing her eyes and taking her final pulses of pleasure from their entwined hands.

———

SHIT. Shit, fuck, and damn. Van's reflection looked back at her from the mirror, and goddamn did she look well-fucked. Hair crazy, face lit with afterglow, lips still a little kiss-swollen. Scoring with a woman like Willa should've made her feel like a goddess, but instead Van was freaking out. Freaking. The fuck. Out.

How could she have just banged Nate's baby sister? That was a thing she had decided very specifically she would not do, and here she was looking—and feeling—thoroughly lady-loved. Nate wasn't the kind of big brother who would lose his shit about his little sister being a sexual being. But she wasn't sure if that would extend to his bestie being the person his sister was having the sexy times with. She'd always been *Nate's* friend, and she could see how her becoming…intimate with Willa would feel like she was betraying that.

Even though Van was kind of a turd about keeping up with the details of people's other people, she did know one thing for certain: Nate adored Willa, and if this ended badly, he was going to be very unhappy with her and in more than a using-her-full-name kind of way. The thought made her sick to her stomach. Nate was one of the people she loved most in the whole world, and no woman was worth losing that.

Not even sex-mussed Willa who was drowsing in her bed at this very second. Shit. But there was some good news here, right? This didn't have to be the end of the world. In a few weeks, she'd be headed back to Charlottesville and Willa would be headed back to Stanford, and that would be that. Being on opposite sides of the country didn't exactly encourage long-term relationships.

This could be a camp fling. Enjoy each other for a few weeks, and when the cabins were all closed up, they'd move on with their lives. No need to pick out china patterns or some shit.

And if this was just going to be a casual sexing thing, Nate wouldn't even have to know. At all. Ever. Yeah, that was good.

That solution gave her the confidence to uncurl her fingers from where they'd developed a death-grip on their bathroom sink and turn on the water. The cold felt good on her face and further helped her chill. She could do this. Having limited-time flings with people was one of life's great pleasures. At Comic-Con and academic conferences, she looked forward to getting into some attractive woman's pants—why should summer camp be any different? And if that super-fine woman happened to be Willa Carter? Did that really matter so much?

She'd just go with no. Not that that stopped her from crossing her fingers behind her back as she tiptoed back to where Willa was sound asleep in Van's bed. Though a little voice piped up when she climbed in beside her and just had to cuddle up because the bed was so damn small, she ignored it. Maybe the rest of this summer would turn out better than she'd thought.

10

Tonight was all hands on deck. Heather usually demanded it when it was a big night, and tonight was huge. The only people who were excused from the festivities were Willa and Van so they could do more planning for their eighties extravaganza. Aquitaine was arriving in less than three weeks, and they were finalizing plans.

Willa was sad to be missing tonight, in all honesty, because Prom Redo sounded like a blast, but a night alone with Van? Even if they were working? She could be down with that. Who was she kidding? She was hoping going down would in fact be a part of this evening.

Willa toweled off and threw on a shirtdress. When she was presentable, she plopped down at her desk, cracked open her tin of sunflower seeds, and started poring over her notes. Monday would be trivia night, Tuesday would be *Star Wars* night... Was it getting hot in here or was that the memories from the other night? Whatever it was, Willa took up a page of notes to fan herself with.

Van was lobbying hard for Friday night to be some sort of *Ghostbusters* extravaganza, so Saturday night would be the John

Hughes mash-up ball. Wednesday she was thinking a slumber party with video games, movies, crimping irons, puff paint T-shirts, and friendship bracelets. Which left Thursday.

She turned on her eighties mix to get herself into the groove and racked her brain for one more thing to add to the schedule. Hopefully Van would have more ideas than she did, but then again, she usually did, irritatingly smart woman.

Van should be back any second now, but in the meantime, she could catch up on some of the journals that had been piling up in her inbox. She couldn't afford to be a month and a half behind her colleagues when she got back, especially knowing she'd get ragged on for her tan.

People who did field research in caves were usually as pale as the sightless creatures they happened upon in the course of their explorations, and being tennis-tanned as she was, Willa was already kind of an anomaly without having spent six weeks at a goddamn summer camp.

Which was fine. She didn't mind the good-natured poking in her department, but she needed to make sure that was all it was. They could tease her all they liked as long as deep down they knew she had earned her place there as surely as they did. It was sometimes an uphill battle to be taken seriously in academia when her original scholarship had been for tennis—it was possible it would've been a good idea to go to a different university where no one knew—but she liked to think she'd proved herself. And it was time to keep proving.

So she tossed another handful of sunflower seeds in her mouth, clicked over to a new window in her browser—once again thankful Van had worked her geek mojo to rig up Wi-Fi for them—and signed into the journal site to get to reading.

———

MOST OF THE TIME, this job was easy-peasy. So easy it was down-right boring on any given day. Which was partly what Van had wanted—an escape. But this was like jumping from the frying pan into…maybe a brick wall that knocked her unconscious. She'd spent the morning updating the website, scheduling social media posts and a newsletter, and then all of a sudden—ka-blow! For some reason, their server had gone haywire and the camp's site was up and down and Heather had freaked.

Van had managed to fix it, finally, and at least she'd been excused from the Prom Redo tonight, which had not been high on her list of things to do. If she was lucky, she could persuade task mistress Willa to engage in some extracurricular activities before or—maybe *and* if she were super-lucky?—after they'd done their planning. Truth be told, this was not her area of expertise. Or anywhere near it.

In some ways, Van was creative; had to be in her field. And to get a PhD—like, hello, original research? That shit was not easy. But the kind of thing Heather and the rest of the staff did all the time… It hurt her head thinking about it. Indeed, her head hurt now on the walk back to the cabin.

Sadly, Willa didn't exactly seem like the type to offer her tea and sympathy. More like the kind of girl who thought all the world's problems could be solved by cutting sugar out of your diet and going for a brisk walk. Van groaned thinking about it and not in the fun way. Maybe if she promised to go for a hike with Willa later, she could get five minutes of resting her head in Willa's lap while Willa's callused fingers massaged her scalp.

There were far worse places to be than Willa's lap for damn sure. Perhaps she could convince Willa of the same…

When she stepped over the threshold of the cabin, Willa was sitting at her desk, a foot propped up on her seat so she could rest her chin on her knee while she looked intently at her laptop. She was all high blonde ponytail and long, tanned limbs, and suddenly tea was the last thing on Van's mind. Though that whole her-head-in-Willa's-lap thing was becoming increasingly appealing.

"Hey, Wills. I thought you might've gotten started without me, but no way could you look that intent if you were watching *The Goonies* or something."

Willa shook her head, ponytail dancing around her shoulders. "No. Definitely not anything fun like that. I was reading a journal article about plate subduction."

Yep, that would leave Van cross-eyed as well. Willa stood and stretched, reaching her fingers up toward the ceiling, her long, lean body on full display, the hem of her dress rising temptingly high, her breasts straining at the snug fabric that kept them hidden from view. For sure at some point this evening, that dress was coming off.

When Willa had finished a series of movements that had Van wondering when the last time she'd even touched her own toes was, she turned to Van and wrinkled her pert little nose.

"So would you mind terribly if we went for a walk first before we get down to business? Sometimes moving helps me think, and my brain is, like, bustified from all these journal articles."

Walking was not as good as stripping Willa here and now, but it was far better than sitting down at Willa's neat-as-a-pin desk and trying to get something done. How could the girl think when everything around her was so…clean? Where did all her inspiration come from? Out of thin air?

"Sure, we can go for a walk. As long as we avoid the boathouse. I don't want to get sucked into that."

"Agreed. Actually, I found something on a trail run the other day I thought you might like to see."

"Oh, yeah?"

Van couldn't imagine what that thing might be, unless it were a downed UFO, which would be frigging awesome, but Willa would've totally reported that to the appropriate authorities like some sane person, so probably not. But the way her eyes sparkled and the corner of her mouth pulled up, Van was looking forward to it anyhow.

A few minutes later found her tromping through the woods, and hell if she knew how Willa was navigating. Must be some shit they taught at Girl Scout camp, because Van sure as fuck couldn't tell one tree from another. So she followed Willa through the forest and tried to keep her concerns to herself. There were, after all, people who enjoyed this nature thing, though for the life of her she couldn't understand why. The invention of "inside" was one of the greatest innovations of humankind as far as she was concerned.

Luckily, it wasn't too long until Willa slowed and pointed to a copse of trees to her right. "Through there."

What choice did Van have but to follow?

Once they'd elbowed their way through some branches, Willa threw her arms out and proclaimed, "Tah-dah!"

What the hell was she... Oh.

There was a small pool surrounded by rocks, and in the cooling air of the late summer evening, steam rolled off of it. Steam? This was a—

"It's a hot spring. How cool is that?"

Willa kicked off her sandals and sat on the edge of the pool, dipping her feet in, the water reaching up to her knees while the hem of her dress settled mid-way up her thighs.

"Super-cool." And it was. An actual hot spring this close to camp? "Does anyone else know about it?"

"I can't imagine they don't. It's not far. Although, if you're not looking for it, you might never find it."

"Or if you're not insane and go for runs in the middle of the woods at the ass-crack of dawn."

"Or that," Willa conceded, kicking her feet, making splashes and ripples in the water. "You coming or what?"

She wished. An orgasm right now would be phenomenal, but Willa probably hadn't brought her out here for sex. So she could settle for shucking her shoes and socks and rolling up her pant legs until her calves were bared. She sat next to Willa, enjoying the companionable silence between them until Willa broke it and broke it hard.

"Do you think people do it out here?"

Dammit. Van almost choked on nothing at all, and Willa pounded her on the back a few times.

Once she'd recovered, she pitched Willa what she hoped was a winning smile. "People do it everywhere."

"That's true."

They sat there for a few minutes, energy and attraction crackling between them, the easy silence gone. When Van couldn't ignore it anymore, she made a joke. "Is that what you brought me here for? Doing it?"

This thing with Willa was brand-new. If it wasn't, Van would've been able to read her better, not had to ask. Willa laughed, but didn't say no. *She didn't say no.* Hint taken.

Van slid her legs out of the water and swung onto Willa's lap, careful not to fall backward into the water. Grace was not her middle name, but she could pull this off.

"That's it, isn't it? You brought me out here with licentious intentions, didn't you? I can't believe it. Here I thought we were supposed to be working—" That was why Heather had given them permission to get out of tonight's activities after all. Not for Van to be slipping her arms around Willa's neck and leaning in close to press their breasts together. "—and you're trying to seduce me, an impressionable young woman."

"Pfft." Willa's dismissive noise was adorable, and her cheeks had definitely gone pinker than usual. "Sometimes sex makes me think better."

Which wasn't an idea entirely without merit. After all, sometimes when Van was struggling with a particularly difficult problem, she could get further by distracting herself with something totally engaging and completely immersive than she could by banging her head up against the brick wall of her issue.

"Then I guess we have to. For science and, you know, our jobs. It's our sworn duty."

Willa was giggling now, her face buried in her hands. "When you put it that way, it sounds ridiculous."

"Nah. This is completely rational."

To prove it, Van stood up and unclipped her overalls, shoving them to her feet and pulling her long-sleeved MIT T-shirt over her head.

———

OH MY GOD. She'd been kidding. Sort of. But never did she think Van would actually strip down bare-ass naked in the middle of the woods, especially knowing how close they actually were to camp, even though it felt a million miles away.

And yet there she was, in all her glory. And she was glorious. In all her fantasies about Van, never had Willa thought of Van's body as lush, and now she had to wonder why. Van was soft and beautifully shaped, her hips and thighs round, even her stomach was a smooth plane of invitation. Van had made the mistake of getting undressed a few steps away from the hot spring, so her skin turned to gooseflesh as she made a break for it, wrapping her arms under her small breasts tipped with hardening brown nipples.

At least Van had enough sense to climb into the spring carefully instead of cannon-balling like it appeared she might. Once she was in the pool, the water lapping just below her shoulders, she looked up at Willa. "You know, I've never been a big fan of doing it in water, but I can see why people would think it was a good idea."

"Same. It's the moisture thing, isn't it? You expect it to make things all hot and wet and slick, but what it actually does is..."

Van moved closer, and damn if Willa could remember what she was going to say. She was far too intent on Van's hands coming out of the water to land on Willa's knees and part them. "It does succeed in making some things slippery, though."

Which is when Van's fingers trailed up her thighs and Willa lost her ability to think in coherent sentences at all. Van's shoulders and biceps were plump and her breasts were just above the waterline. She was mouth-watering, simply delicious. And she had an intent look on her face that made other parts of Willa just as wet.

When Van tugged at the sides of her underwear, Willa tipped her hips up and allowed Van to slide them all the way down her legs. Willa tried to keep her feet out of the water so the scrap of cotton wouldn't get wet—fine, wetter—but wasn't terribly successful. When she'd settled, her ass was bare against the warmed rocks. Strange, but pleasurable.

"Come here." Van tugged at her knees until Willa's butt was wavering over the edge of the pool, and then, then... "Lean back."

Oh, my. Willa did as she was told, leaning back and letting Van scoot her even farther off the edge, sliding her sundress up until she wasn't decent. Nope, not at all. Her breath came faster and she was feeling hot and cold all at once. Maybe dizzy.

"You look like a wanton little water nymph, you know that?"

Willa could only whimper as Van kissed the inside of one knee, sending tingles straight to her core. And kept kissing until she was nearly to the place Willa wanted her to kiss most, and then she was gone again, scooping the heated water over Willa's spread thighs, making her shiver with sensory overload.

The hot water and the cool air, the hard rocks covered by the soft fallen leaves and pine needles, and the spine-tingling intimacy of having Van staring into her very core were nearly her undoing. She was determined to hold out, though, because this was bound to get better.

It did when Van threaded her fingers through Willa's own and held their hands to the sides of Willa's thighs while Van's mouth laid a trail of kisses up Willa's opposite leg.

"Beautiful girl," Van crooned while she loved the inside of Willa's thigh, and every sensual nerve in Willa's body lit up. Her breasts ached and she arched her back, even widened the spread of her legs though she knew it would make her look even more... how had Van put it? Wanton? So be it. There was no one here to see her be so shameless, and if Camp Firefly Falls was about anything, it was grown-up fun and games. Although this felt sweet too. Like it was about more than just pleasure.

The thought slipped away as quickly as it had come, and as Willa abandoned any sense of decorum she ought to have, she started to beg. "Please, Van, please. I need your mouth."

Pressing kisses to the juncture of where hip met thigh, Van teased her relentlessly with lips and tongue and teeth. "You have it."

"Not where I want it."

"Where do you want it?"

Everywhere. She wanted Van's mouth everywhere, forever. But in the interest of expediency, because she hadn't gone completely senseless from the sensual havoc Van was wreaking on her, she decided to be more direct. "On my pussy. I want your mouth on my pussy. Please."

She expected a teasing response, maybe some gentle mocking about her complete and utter lack of control, but what she got was a swirling of Van's tongue around her clit, and then lips closing around that sensitive, swollen bud to suck.

"Fuck. Jesus, Van, your mouth."

Then Van's tongue was...inside her. The shallow penetration wasn't as satisfying as a cock or other things designed to make a woman feel good and full, but the way she could *move*. Willa couldn't help but toss her head from side to side, even knowing she'd be picking leaves out of her hair for days.

Worth. It.

When Van returned her attentions to Willa's clit and sucked before worrying it softly with her teeth, Willa was a goner. She didn't even try to swallow her cries of ecstasy.

After licking her through every last pulse of aftershock, Van moved closer still, her arms resting on top of Willa's spread thighs while Willa could do nothing but try to find her breath while she looked at the stars coming out in the darkening sky. Jesus.

"You put on quite the show there, Wills."

Willa's lips curled into a satiated smile, but then something nagged at the back of her brain. It wasn't panic, though it could've been—camp wasn't far away, but she was confident it was far enough they wouldn't have heard her. Probably. But show, show...

She sat up hastily and jabbed a finger into Van's self-satisfied face. "That's it!"

"Uh, what?" It wasn't often Willa got to see Van perplexed, so she took a mental snapshot and tucked it away before she continued.

"A show. That's what we can do on Thursday night. An eighties talent show. Lipsyncing, skits, whatever else people sign up for. The campers will have enough time to prepare. You could even mention it in their pre-arrival newsletter, and they could pick up props and stuff before they even get here. It'll be fabulous."

Van looked up at her, and suddenly Willa burned with embarrassment. "Oh my god, I'm so sorry. I totally ruined the mood, didn't I? That was the best head I've ever gotten, and here I am going on about a talent show. Do you hate me?"

Van shook her head as she bit her lip. "I don't, because you're frigging adorable when you're all gung-ho about something, but I'm not going to lie. I'd kinda hoped there would be a longer lag time between the sex and the idea-having."

"I'm the worst."

"No, you're not. Not even close. Let's go back to camp and get all this stuff down before you forget anything."

"But—"

"It's fine." Van's dark eyes weren't lying. She wasn't angry. She might have even been charmed, although Willa would settle for amused. "We'll go back to the cabin, write all this down, and send it to Heather, and when she tells us how much she loves it, we can celebrate. Besides, you know orgasming isn't the only way to get pleasure out of sex, right?"

"Sure…" She'd had pleasurable sex without coming. For intimacy, for comfort, for closeness, for giving pleasure to her partner. Sometimes for exertion's or anger's sake, for that matter. "But I do think it's best when there are climaxes involved."

Van snorted. "I will keep that in mind for the future, but I assure you I enjoyed myself very much just now."

Then she was climbing out of the pool, using her BB-8 underwear to get as much water off of her as she could before pulling on her shirt and overalls and shoving the damp handful of orange and white fabric into one pocket and Willa's underwear into the other.

Willa was about to protest—was Van seriously taking a souvenir of her conquest?—but then Van grinned, showing her perfect white teeth. "You don't have any pockets in that dress. So unless you want to carry your wet undies back, bunched up in your hand…"

Oh god. Willa's face flamed. No, no, she did not want to do that. Just in case they did run into someone on their way back to the cabin, which would totally be her luck. Nor did she want to slide the spring-damp cotton up her legs and try not to squirm all the way back to the cabin. So she mutely shook her head and Van's grin didn't dim a lumen.

"All right then, let's go."

11

"I'M SORRY, Van. I love your idea, but laser tag equipment is expensive, too much to spend for one night. How about we put it on the list next year? Then we'd be able to plan more events around it to justify the cost."

Van almost felt bad for Heather, who looked as though she wanted to offer Van a lollipop and a BB-8 Band-Aid. Which Van would totally accept, although she'd prefer a cookie and dammit, most of all, to be able to execute her brilliant idea.

The thing was, though, Van wasn't one to give up easily. If at all. If she thought about it hard enough, she could make this happen and it would be epic. Camp legend. Also, chasing Willa through the woods had a certain appeal. Not that she'd be able to keep up with her, but maybe Willa would take it easy on her?

The corner of Van's mouth curled up. Not a chance. That's when the lightbulb went off.

"So, okay. I get that you can't outfit the entire camp in brand-new laser tag gear—especially since you'd probably use it a few times a season at most and the rest of the time it would sit in a shed getting spider-infested. But what if I provided you with the equipment?"

Heather looked skeptical, and frankly Van couldn't blame her. She wasn't entirely confident she could pull this off either, especially given they only had two weeks before the Aquitaine session started, but dammit, it was worth a shot.

"How exactly would you do that?"

Oh, how she wished there hadn't been a pause there. She could still pull this out of the fire, though. The answer was—as it so often was—she was going to have to engineer the shit out of this. *Game on.* "If I can find enough spare parts from old video game systems and the swap table at the dump, I bet I could cobble together some pretty sick proton packs."

Heather's eyebrows crunched together in confusion. Right, she was talking to a non-geek. Better rephrase. "I think I can find enough spare parts on e-Bay and stuff to put together the guns and the receivers. We could have two teams: ghosts and Ghostbusters. Maybe the ghosts wouldn't have guns, because I don't know if I could rig up that many in such a short time, but they could have slime balls and if one of the 'busters got hit, they'd be out. Please, Heather? At least let me try. If I can't pull it off—" *please let me be able to pull it off* "—I'll run a different evening activity, like making Stay Puft Marshmallow Man S'mores or something."

She could tell Heather was on the fence by the way she chewed her lip and crossed her arms, but she could also tell Heather wanted to say yes. Because of course she did. Who in their right mind wouldn't want to play *Ghostbusters* laser tag? And Heather loved themes. Fucking *loved* them.

Van made her best puppy-dog eyes in hopes that would push Heather over the edge.

"Ugh, fine. You win."

Van didn't even try to hide her whoop of delight. It came spilling out of her mouth, and her arms went up in a V. V for motherfucking victory. Heather quickly cut off her celebrating with a finger waving in her face.

"If you don't get this done, you need to figure out an alternative. I like your s'mores idea, but maybe we could have something else too? Like a haunted house?"

Van choked on a gag. No freaking way. She would rather die than have to put together a haunted house, but she wasn't going to admit that to Heather. So rigged-up proton packs it was going to be. Now to scour the internet for leftover *Duck Hunt* guns and see if someone else had already figured out how to make this work. Also she'd need to dig out her soldering iron. Which conveniently was somewhere in the cabin, she just didn't quite know where. What she did know was to never leave home without it. Van Thompson: Engineering the shit out of…well, shit since longer than she'd like to think about.

"Uh, I'll think on it and get back to you with a few ideas. Thank you. You will not regret this."

Then she booked it out of Heather's office before she could change her mind. Now to put her plan into motion. Her first stop was the same as it always was. She dragged her phone out of her pocket and pressed the first number in her speed dial. To be fair, she hadn't dialed it as recently as she should have. Nate was still in Connecticut, taking full advantage of his company's loosey-goosey culture, and as awesome as the Carters were, they weren't peers. It's possible she'd been avoiding Nate, though.

Possible.

But if Van just steered clear of mentioning Willa, everything would be fine. It's not like they usually had a summit on Nate's baby sister when they talked, so why should things be any different now? Nate picked up on the second ring.

"'Sup?"

"I have the world's most awesome idea, but I'm going to need your help to pull it off."

She could practically hear Nate perk up on the other side of the line. He'd decided to hang out at his parents' rather than go back up to Boston, and she couldn't really blame him. Mr. Carter was a way better cook than Nate was, and Mrs. Carter made killer drinks. Despite those perks, he was maybe regretting that decision some since he was bored as fuck. She could tell by the number of *Sheep Leap* invitations he'd sent her on social media. Yeah, he was working some, but there was no water cooler culture at the homestead. Hopefully she could turn his desperation to her advantage, and when he responded, she knew she had him.

"I'm all ears."

"Well, you'd better be all fingers in a second because this is going to take some serious google-fu."

"Got it, boss. Whaddya need?"

"DIY gear for *Ghostbusters* laser tag?" Van wasn't usually hesitant, didn't phrase declarations as questions, but even she knew this was a big ask. And when Nate was silent for a few seconds, she thought she'd lost him. "Nate?"

"Sorry, just picking my brains up off the floor because you just blew my mind. That's going to be sick, and I can't believe I'm missing it." There were some curses which Van assumed were directed at his busted leg.

"If I can pull it off, yeah, but at this point, it's kind of a big if."

"So what are you thinking? *Duck Hunt* guns would be perfect, but the receivers are a little trickier…"

They spent a few minutes brainstorming, and when they had a good base to build on, Nate turned their chat to a place Van did not want to go. "So are you being nicer to Willa?"

Did giving her shuddering orgasms count? "Um, yes?"

"Why did you say it like that? If you're still being a dick—"

"I'm not. Swear." Van would do anything to get them off this topic of conversation. "So how many *Duck Hunt* guns have you found so far?"

"Whoa, you are not getting off that easily." There was a super-inappropriate yo' sister joke in there, but Van kept her mouth shut and waited. "I need evidence. Tell me something nice you did for Willa."

She sure as fuck wasn't going to tell him about all the sex they were having, so it would have to be something else. Something nice so Nate would be satisfied, but not so nice that he'd be suspicious. "We...practiced our cosplay for *Star Wars* night and I did her hair."

There. That sounded innocent enough, and it was met with a begrudging grunt of approval. Thank goodness for that, because with everything else that was going on, Van could not afford to be short a best friend.

"Good. Keep it up."

Try and stop me. "Will do. Now, about those Duck Hunt guns..."

It was with a profound sense of relief Van listened to Nate rattle off the sources he'd already found and then start rhapsodizing about how they might equip everyone in camp with receivers. She didn't want talking to Nate to feel like picking her way through a minefield, but she could hold out until the end of the summer when everything would go back to normal and Nate would never need to know about her and Willa.

———

WILLA SENT another easy lob over the net toward Heather while they had their now-traditional pre-lunch tennis match. Well, more of a lesson because while Heather was improving, she was no match for Willa. As evidenced by her missing Willa's latest shot along the line.

Heather jogged after the offending ball and then tossed it to Willa. "So I had a nice chat with Van this morning."

"About what?" Willa lined up her serve, conscious to make it an easy one. It was good practice anyhow, made her focus more on placement than on force.

Heather managed to return this one with a nice deep shot that actually left Willa scrambling. No way had Heather done that on purpose, but Willa didn't mind the challenge. No, it felt good to stretch her legs and put some hustle in her bustle.

"Ghostbuster laser tag of all things. She's got a real head of steam about this. Think she can pull it off?"

They settled into an easy rhythm of batting the ball back and forth, and once it was established, Willa answered. "If Van says she can pull something off, then she can. She's crazy smart and she works really hard."

Heather missed again, and as she was trotting back with the ball, she gave Willa a sly look. "What are you, president of the Van fan club?"

A bit of a blush came into Willa's cheeks, hopefully covered up by her sun and workout-flushed face. "No. I mean, she's great, but…"

"But what?"

Yeah, Heather had perfected that faux-innocent, intimating expression.

"But nothing."

"Mmhmm."

"What's that supposed to mean?"

"It means that you two have been looking at each other all starry-eyed for the past couple of weeks, and I thought it might be more than just a mutual admiration society. Or bunkmates. Is there something going on between the two of you?"

Heather took advantage of Willa's distractedness to get her

first—and likely only—shot past Willa. She grinned and jogged to the side of the court, picking up her water and taking a few gulps.

Hmm. Should she tell Heather? And if so, how much? It's not like there was some kind of rule against fraternizing between employees—that would've been awfully hypocritical on Heather and Michael's part—but Heather was her boss. Only for a few more weeks, though, and she was dying to dish to someone.

"Okay, okay," Willa said as she trotted over to join Heather. They should probably wrap things up anyhow so they could grab lunch—it was a barbecue today, and Meg made ribs to die for. Also a kale, carrot, raisin, and walnut salad she usually served with them, so all together, Willa was a very happy girl. Not to mention that things were going so very well with Van. "We're sort of a thing."

Heather whistled and Willa rolled her eyes, but that familiar flush crept over her face again.

"Only sort of?"

On the one hand, Willa didn't want to give in to Heather's egging on, but on the other hand, she wanted someone to squee with. No one at Stanford had ever met Van, so they wouldn't understand, and while she wasn't averse to telling Nate about her dating life, she wasn't quite ready to spill the beans about Van yet. Soon, though, because shit was getting real and Nate did not like to be the last one to know.

"Fine. We're definitely a thing, okay? We're not talking bed linens to put on our registry or what preschool our kids are going to go to, but I am starting to plan when we'll be able to see each other once we go back to school. It'll be a little rough navigating two academic calendars on opposite coasts, but I think we'll be able to handle it."

"Whoa. That's pretty serious. I didn't know you were thinking about 'The Future.'"

The way Heather verbally capitalized those words caught Willa up short. No, they hadn't exactly discussed it, but what else could all this mean? It was more than a fling for sure. But the way Heather was eyeing her... "What?"

"You might want to think about making sure Van is planning for the future too. That is, if you haven't already."

Well, duh. Willa wasn't going to go back to the cabin and buy a year's worth of plane tickets, but she had maybe, possibly, written out a list of possible long weekends they could see each other. Of course, that would depend on their class schedules and department obligations and all that, but wasn't it obvious? It certainly was to Willa...

"Of course she is. We've talked about next year." Not exactly specifically about their relationship, but about classes and stuff. So Van must be thinking about it. Of course she was. Willa needed to stop letting Heather making her crazy. "So there will be planes involved, but that's fine. Plus, there's always skyping and talking on the phone—"

"And sexting."

"Heather!" Willa's eyes bugged as she whipped her head around to look at her boss.

"Sorry, I just always wanted to say that. But really, that's great. Have you told Nate yet?" Willa sunk her teeth into her bottom lip, and Heather laughed. "I'm taking that as a no?"

"No, but I will soon."

"Do you think he'll be mad?"

"No." Willa shook the hair out of her face and pushed the sweat-sticky strands back further before taking another sip of water. Her brother wasn't one of those guys who wanted to lock his little sister in a tower and keep her there until she was forty. "He might be a little worried because it's like his two favorite people's happiness eggs all in one basket, you know? But I don't think he'll be worried after he sees us together."

"You are an awfully cute couple."

Willa curtsied her thanks and gave Heather a quick goodbye hug. Her boss had to run so she could meet up with Michael for lunch, and she had to book it back to the cabin to grab a Band-Aid to put over a rapidly forming blister.

On the way, she broke out her cell and called her brother. "Nate the Great, how's it going?"

"I have a bendy straw, a Tipsy Arnie, and a new project to keep me busy. I'm good. Also, you're the second Camp Firefly Falls staff member to call me today. Is Heather not keeping you guys busy enough? Because I've got to tell you, that doesn't sound like her at all."

"No, she's definitely keeping me on my toes. I'm just on my way to the cabin to grab a Band-Aid before I get lunch. Ribs today!"

Nate groaned. "Seriously? You're going to tease me like that? You're a cruel one, Willa the Killa."

"Oh my god, you're a dork." But he was her big brother, and he was the best kind of goofball. She wouldn't have him any other way. But that did make her wonder... "Who else called you?"

"Van did. She roped me into her *Ghostbusters* laser tag venture. I am desperately jealous of you guys getting up to shenanigans in the woods."

Willa had to cover her mouth so Nate wouldn't hear the strangled sound she made. Yeah, there definitely had been shenanigans in the woods, but not the kind he was thinking of. She cleared her throat and then, in the coolest voice she could manage, asked, "Did she say anything about me?"

"Who? Van?" There was an uncouth slurp on the other end of the line, and Willa rolled her eyes. No wonder her brother hadn't found someone to settle down with yet. His manners were somewhat lacking, despite their mother's best efforts. "Not really. Why?"

Not really? What was that supposed to mean? It was a simple question that should've yielded a yes or no answer. But clearly, Van hadn't mentioned them dating because Nate would've called Willa, not waited for her to call him. Okay. That was fine. She probably just wasn't ready yet. It's not like they were carrying on some covert affair and she was Van's shameful secret. No need to freak. All in good time.

"No reason."

"Is she still giving you a hard time? She said you were getting along better, but if that's not true, you give me the word, and I'll give her a tongue-lashing."

Pinching her nose shut was the only way Willa could stop the snort this time. She would much rather it be herself giving Van a tongue-lashing, but Nate really did not need to know that level of detail.

"No, no. It's fine. We're on, um, much better terms." *Fucking terms.* "No need for you to intervene."

"Okay, good. Van is great, but sometimes it takes her a while to warm up to new people, you know? And I know you're not *new* new, but you've never hung out as adults, so it's different than when she basically used to live at our house when we were kids."

Yes, yes, it was. And thank heaven for that. She needed to get off the phone before she completely lost her shit. Plus, she was skipping up their cabin steps so she'd have to hang up soon anyhow. That Band-Aid wasn't going to cover her blister by itself.

"I get it. And hey, I gotta go, but I'll talk to you soon, okay?"

"Yeah, yeah. Go off and live your glamorous camp life. I'm going to have another drink and then try to figure out how Van can mass-produce DIY laser tag equipment."

Because that could only end well. Nothing bad could possibly come out of drunk Nate fooling around with electronics. "Don't be stupid. Play with electricity and *then* drink."

12

THE AQUITAINE CREW had arrived the night before to a Camp Firefly Falls welcome with a full staff decked out in neon and crimped hair, which they'd been delighted by, and after a full day of team-building activities, trivia night had been a rousing success. Thank Holtzmann, because she and Willa had busted their asses on this week and they'd been abuzz with anticipation.

It was gratifying to see people enjoying something she'd had a hand in. And wow, did she love to see Willa get all het up. Competition in academia was quieter, more subtle, if still as brutal as the competition in sports, and Van was as competitive as anyone, hence the PhD in only four years. There was something about seeing Willa get all buzzed, her eyes alight with competition, that made her wish academia was the same.

During trivia, Willa and Van's teams had been neck-and-neck for most of the game, answering questions about what year in the future had Michael J. Fox actually gone back to and what model car had Cameron's dad owned in *Ferris Bueller's Day Off*.

Willa was all high-fives and smiles, even doing sexy-as-fuck victory dances when her team scored a tough question. Unbeknownst to the rest of the people there, there was more on the line than a personal popcorn maker as a prize; Willa and Van had their own bet on the outcome. After routing Van's team in the equivalent of Final Jeopardy, Willa was surely plotting how best to collect.

As she headed back to their cabin, Van was fantasizing about the same. Willa was on clean-up duty, so she had their shared space to herself for a while, and while she'd usually take advantage to play a game or to catch up on journals or email, she decided to tidy up a bit.

Not that Willa had said anything and Van did her best to keep her mess on her side of the room, but Willa would probably be pleasantly surprised if the cabin was cleaner when she came back. Also, if Van were being totally honest with herself, the swamp was getting out of control. Even for her tastes.

So she set to picking some things off the floor, putting clothes in the closet or in the laundry, books on her desk, and other stuff...wherever she could find room for it. She hadn't needed to bring so much stuff with her, but dammit she liked to be comfortable and nothing made her happier than her collections, so they traveled with her a lot.

She was about to set a Rey figurine on an empty slice of shelf when her phone pinged. Ugh, the university. Checking the message didn't make her feel any better. More paperwork. She was used to documenting things—every scientist worth their salt was—but the university had brought the art of bureaucracy to a whole new level. A level of hell, to be precise.

This form had to be signed in triplicate and returned to three offices; changing the scheduling of a class required not only the approval of the department chair, registrar, and space planning office, but also their respective great aunts. Also, the grant needed not only a detailed description of what the funds would be used for, but also a DNA sample and the size of your left shoe.

If she could spend that time doing her research instead of

dealing with all this bullshit, she could be so much further along. Also, while she'd always been more interested in the theoretical aspects of her field, the practical applications were starting to nag at her brain more and more often. Mostly when she was doing more goddamn administrative work. Coincidence? She had to think not.

What the hell was that supposed to mean? Some of her class-mates had felt the siren song of the private sector, lured by money, more flexibility in terms of geography, and in some cases, more resources at their disposal than Van could even dream of. Though she'd publicly congratulated them, in private she'd rolled her eyes. What a waste.

Finest minds in a generation, and what were they being used for? Essentially building a better mouse trap as far as she was concerned. Not True Science™. Which she was now realizing had been a super-dickish attitude to have, but one she'd come by honestly from her advisor and other people she'd worked with closely. To switch to the other side now? No, not a possibility.

Academia was where she was meant to be, where she'd always wanted to be, and perhaps most importantly, where she actually was. The thought of starting over from square one made her want to puke up all the citrus and truffle-oil popcorn she'd consumed during trivia.

Thankfully, her tetchiness was interrupted by the opening of the cabin door. Willa. Dear god, yes. Nothing better to snap her out of this slump than a sexy blonde who owned her ass for the night.

Willa grinned at her from the door. "I've got to take a shower because I didn't get a chance between my last lesson and trivia but then I have plans for you."

Yeah, that feeling was every erotic nerve in her body perking up. Van didn't want to sit here twiddling her thumbs while she waited for Willa. Then she'd talk herself into a funk again, and she wanted to be happy, wanted to enjoy.

But even fooling around with Willa wasn't unqualified fun times. She felt shitty about lying to Nate, about talking to him less than usual so she wouldn't have to lie, and Willa was her reason for doing that. But she could let it ride for another week, right? That's all she had to get through, and then their fling would end amicably and things could go back to the way they were, just with more orgasms than she'd previously had. She shook it off, because she was going to carpe the fuck out of this diem and out of Willa as well.

"Mind if I join you?"

Willa stripped her T-shirt over her head and stood there in a sports bra and her tennis skirt. What had Van done in her life to deserve this? Must've been something good, because goddamn.

"In the shower?"

"Yeah."

"Um, okay. It's not very big."

No, it wasn't, but luckily Van didn't take up all that much room. "True. Don't worry, I'll make myself useful."

By the way her eyebrow ticked up and her lips curled at the corners, Willa liked the sound of that. "Well, when you put it like that. Sure, gimme a minute."

That she could do. Soon she heard the shower turn on, and Willa poked her head out the door. "Coming?"

"I sure as heck hope so," Van muttered under her breath. She stripped off her own clothes on the way, not even having enough patience to wait until she got into the bathroom. Willa was already in the shower stall, tipping her head back under the stream of the shower, looking like some teenager's wet dream.

Water sluiced down her lithe, muscular body, the spray forming rivulets that called attention to all of Willa's curves, and Van couldn't wait to get her hands on them. Luckily, she didn't have to. She opened the door to the stall and stepped in, trying not to crowd Willa, but also unable to avoid touching her. Gee, darn.

She'd showered that morning and it wasn't as though being a desk jockey demanded multiple scrub downs, but when in Rome... Van shrugged and grabbed her bar of soap, lathering up while Willa washed her long hair. She'd like to do it for Willa, but didn't offer. Van wasn't sure she'd be able to do the best job, what with being shorter than Willa. Sure, she'd be able to stretch and get her fingers to the top of her scalp, but would it really be satisfying for either of them? Better done in a bathtub where they were on more equal footing.

Yeah, for whenever they could be in a tub together. Jesus. That was never going to happen. No future here, folks, and that was for the best.

What Van did feel more than comfortable doing was keeping hold of the soap and rubbing it between her hands until there was a veritable froth of bubbles going up to her wrists. Those bubbles? They were meant for Willa.

She set the soap on the small ledge and reached out for Willa's back—an innocuous place to start. She soaped Willa from hip to neck, careful not to get any of the lather into Willa's freshly rinsed hair. Then, on to Willa's muscular arms and the sides of her ribcage, and then...Van's slick hands ran over Willa's flared hips, her thumbs tilted in toward Willa's spine, and as she went lower, the cleft of her ass.

The woman seriously had one of the finest bottoms known to mankind, and Van sent a silent thank you up to whatever deity had declared Willa would play tennis, the skirts the better to show it off with. She spent far longer than strictly necessary washing this particular part of Willa's anatomy, and Willa didn't seem to mind, eventually resting her head against the tiles and exhaling softly.

It seemed only right to slide her hands over Willa's hips to wash the front of her body—didn't want to do a half-assed job, after all—so across her hipbones and flat belly, up to her ribcage, and then yes, Willa's heavy breasts, which Van also took her time with. She pinched Willa's hard nipples between her fingers and let them slip through before squeezing and kneading her flesh and pinching her again.

Van didn't think it was her imagination Willa's breathing had quickened, become shallow, and she wanted to turn it into a different sound. She slicked her soapy hands down once again, insinuating her fingers between Willa's legs, to which Willa responded by setting her feet farther apart and arching her back. All right, then.

It wasn't a hardship to work Willa's clit with leisurely circles, and soon Van found herself pressed against Willa's backside. The contact felt damn good, and Van had some pretty filthy ideas of what she could do given the right equipment. She had a feeling Willa wouldn't object to getting fucked that way, but no such luck at the moment. She'd have to settle for other means.

Van went up on tiptoes to grab the showerhead from its mount and brought it down until its spray was directed where her fingers had been. Willa moaned softly and rocked her hips. Good. She'd be content to tease Willa until their water ran cold, but she was also eager to get to the other portion of the evening. So while she wouldn't describe it as rushing, Van moved on with her plan to drive Willa out of her damn mind.

This included threading her hand between Willa's legs and pressing fingers inside her from behind. Delightfully slick and eager, Willa pushed back against her. Between the stimulation of the water from the showerhead and the pumping of Van's fingers inside her, it wasn't long before Willa's interior walls were pulsing around Van's fingers and she was swearing in a completely delightful way.

Taking the showerhead away from where it had been doing its devilish work, Van hung it back in its mount and slid her fingers out from inside Willa. But she wasn't quite ready to let go, so she circled her arms around Willa, who still had her head resting against the tiles, and laid her own forehead between Willa's shoulder blades.

It was pleasurable to both hear and feel Willa's breathing and heartbeat, but they couldn't stay here forever. They would run out of hot water, and that would be a chilly and shocking end to what had been a rather delightful interlude.

Willa must've had the same thought, because she turned in Van's arms and laid a kiss on Van's lips before checking them both for soap. None found, she shut off the water and got towels.

They dried themselves off, but when Van went out to find some clothes, Willa tutted at her. "I don't think so. Your ass is still mine tonight, and believe me, you won't be needing any clothes."

Who the hell was Van to argue with that?

———

THE WOMAN HAD SWAGGER, Willa had to give her that. She would. That, and a whole lot more. She'd had a few ideas of what to do with her prize, but after the shower shenanigans, she was sure. Van was in for a treat.

"On my bed," she instructed as she headed for her bureau. On the way there, she noticed Van's side wasn't quite as cluttered as usual. "Did you clean up?"

Van shrugged a single shoulder as well as she could from where she was lying supine on Willa's bed. "Little bit, while I was waiting for you to get back."

"Looks good." Willa smiled, pleased, because there was no way Van had done that for her own gratification. No, that was all for Willa, and she appreciated it.

Willa turned her attention back to her sock drawer where she rummaged for what she was looking for. Finding it, she drew it out and held it up for Van to see.

"Is that a—"

"Vibrator? Yeah. Don't worry, I clean my toys really well." She had, in fact, purchased this particular vibrator because it was easy to clean. A small seamless bullet connected to the controller by a thin wire.

"Toys?" Van sputtered, with an emphasis on the *s*. "I mean, don't get me wrong I love a woman who packs for everything, but damn."

"Yes, plural, but we'll stick with this one for tonight."

Willa strode over to where Van was waiting for her and didn't waste any time, oh no. She put the vibrator on the cluttered desk and climbed over Van before kissing her thoroughly. Their bare bodies, still warm from the shower, pressed against each other, skin against skin downright decadent. Straddling Van and running her hands through Van's short, dark hair felt unbearably right, as did the way Van rocked her hips up and moaned into Willa's mouth.

As much as Willa would like to take her time, luxuriate in the feel of her fantasy's body against her own, she was also fresh out of patience. So she sat back and took up the vibrator, studying it as though she'd never seen it before. Of course, she had, many times—she and it were in fact intimately acquainted—but this was to tease her creative lover.

She'd always been too shy to incorporate toys with her other partners, but as a fellow scientist, she couldn't imagine Van would mind some experimentation.

"This little friend of mine has varying speeds." Willa flicked the control to set the bullet buzzing, and Van's eyes widened. "So you'll have to help me out with what you like best. Which I may or may not take into account."

She grinned back at a glaring Van before flicking the vibrator off entirely. No need to use up the battery when she had something else in mind first. Fingers were an excellent plan, especially since she wanted to feel Van, become familiar with her before she let the toy come between them. Fun it definitely was, but distancing at the same time, and she craved closeness with this woman.

Willa climbed back and then wedged herself between Van's legs, drinking in the sight of her. Hair as dark as that on her head framed the pink slick core of her, and Willa wanted it all for herself. Maybe sometime she'd taste her, but not today.

She explored Van with her fingers, not failing to notice the way Van's hands were clutched at her side and the tendons of her neck stood out, strained. She was pretty like this, vulnerable and strong at the same time.

"I like how you look," Willa mused out loud, hoping her shy words would make Van feel wanted, beautiful in her own way. "I could touch you all over for hours and never get tired. If you'd let me, I'd like to touch inside of you."

There was a hitch in Van's breathing, and Willa couldn't quite tell why. A hell yes or reluctance? Only one way to find out. "Would that be okay?"

Van opened her tightly shut eyes and looked Willa in the face while Willa continued to explore. She'd stop if Van asked her to, but she didn't want to.

"Penetration…it isn't for me like it is for you. It's not a sensation I enjoy, and it's not something that would help me get off. If you want to, you can because I trust you and I want to make you feel good too, but…" Van's lips pursed tight, and she huffed a sigh through her nose. "Sorry."

"Don't be sorry." Yes, she wanted that experience, but not at the expense of Van's comfort. She really didn't want Van to be sorry—there wasn't anything to apologize for—but she did appreciate Van had felt the teeniest bit bad about not being able to give Willa her heart's desire. And yet Van had trusted her enough to say so. Didn't get much better than that. "It's good information to have. Maybe I will sometime if it's really okay with you, but not tonight. Tonight, I want to drive you crazy. I'm not going to do anything that would interfere with that."

Van smiled, then, looking more bashful than she usually did. "Sounds good to me."

Willa slid her fingers back far enough to gather moisture that had gathered at Van's entrance but then drew it up to circle her clit again and—yes, that was the expression she was looking for.

Van's head dropped back against the pillow, and she made a small, strangled noise. While she was distracted, Willa reached for the vibe and set the control to her side, bringing the bullet to where her fingers danced, laying it against Van's swollen bud before turning it on low. Van's hips bucked, and she gasped, her fingers tightening convulsively in the duvet.

"So penetration bad, but vibration good?"

"You could say that." Van's breathy response to Willa's teasing was all the encouragement she needed to turn the knob on the controller, setting the buzzing higher. Van cried out, the sound music to Willa's ears. So maybe she wasn't quite as confident in bed with women as she was with men, but she didn't think she was doing too badly.

Van's breathing and squirming seemed to have reached a plateau, and Willa wanted to send her higher—send Van right to the moon if she could—so she kicked up the vibe one more time.

That was apparently the magic speed because Van laid her hand over Willa's and canted her hips up, pressing the vibe against her own clit, and then she was done for, hissing through her teeth and making these choked noises that would've concerned her if Willa weren't entirely convinced Van was enjoying herself. But no, this is what Van looked like, sounded like, when she climaxed.

It brought a swell of pleasure to Willa's chest, along with wonder. Also, entirely inappropriately, gratitude to Nate for being stupid enough to break his leg while waterskiing because this never would've happened otherwise. This chance to be with her crush, who felt...right.

Willa flicked the vibe off and set it to the side and leaned down to kiss Van again. When she broke away, Van had a goofy, pleasure-drunk smile on her face. "Maybe I should lose at trivia more often."

13

VAN WAS A PRETTY HARDCORE ATHEIST, but if anything could have convinced her that god did, in fact, exist, it would be the get-up Willa was rocking. There was a whole crowd gathered in front of the boathouse and Van was going to have to talk to them in a minute, but for now, she only had eyes for Willa.

If someone would've told her yesterday that a Slimer costume could be sexy, she would've called bullshit, but Willa had some mad skillz. She was wearing her running shoes, but it looked like she'd custom-made everything else on her body. Neon green knee socks, something that looked, honest-to-god, like one of her tennis skirts dyed an unnatural Day-Glo shade of green. Then came the best part. From her waist to all the way over her head, Willa was encased in what looked like a papier-mâché blob, which for Slimer was On. Point. Willa's tennis-toned arms stuck out the sides, and his mouth was open so she could see Willa's eyes. Heaven help her, the woman had even cut a hole in the back of Slimer's head so her blonde ponytail could stick out. It was all she could do not to drool all over her freshly purchased official *Ghostbusters* regulation jumpsuit.

Heather's voice coming through the megaphone yanked her

back from some pretty inappropriate cosplay imagery that had started playing in her mind.

"Welcome to *Ghostbusters* night at Camp Firefly Falls!"

Cheers went up among all the campers and staff, most of whom were decked out as either 'busters or ghosts. Some looked like zombies, but Van wasn't going to be particular. They could be ghost zombies. Yeah.

"Tonight's offerings include both the 2016 and the 1984 versions of the movie playing on loop in the lodge, Stay Puft s'mores at the firepit, and the highlight of the evening: *Ghostbusters* laser tag. Now I'll turn it over to Van Thompson, the mastermind behind all this paranormal fun and the—no shit—engineer of all this equipment."

She gestured to the DIY proton packs, harnesses that had the receivers, and satchels packed with slime balls. The crowd oohed and aahed, and pride swelled in Van's chest. The only time she was comfortable being the center of attention was when she was in front of a lecture hall. There was an element of embarrassment in there somewhere, and she was sure her cheeks were pink, but mostly she was...happy.

Heather handed her the megaphone, and she hefted the thing up to explain the rules.

"Everyone will grab a receiver and strap it on—'busters are going to grab a proton pack, ghosts will grab a satchel. 'Busters, if you shoot someone and their harness lights up, that's a hit, and they're out. Ghosts, your bags are chock full of slime balls and a paintball pistol. Shoot them at the nearest target, and if they hit, the cartridge will bust open and splatter glow-in-the-dark paint all over them."

She waited for someone to sound the alarm about this not being a fair fight or that this wasn't real laser tag equipment, but some jury-rigged stuff that looked like it had come out of someone's garage. But no one seemed to mind the firepower wasn't exactly even and it was clearly DIY tech.

"Last one standing wins bragging rights, plus the right to slime any CFF staff person they choose."

The roar that went up in the crowd was awesome. The Aquitaine group had proved to be very enthusiastic. Never had Van thought she'd hear that kind of noise, and for her. She worked hard and got recognition for that work, but it was in the staid halls of academia where credit came in the form of pieces of paper, journal acceptances, and being awarded grants. Not these visceral, human roars of approval. She envied Willa for a second, who must hear that on a regular basis. Van had always thought sport was a foolish pursuit, but she could see how this kind of feedback could drive someone to the pursuit of excellence.

———

WILLA BOUNCED on the balls of her feet, same way she would if she were getting ready to face down an opponent's serve. She was ready for this. She might not have a racquet in her hand, but she was going to rule this game and slime the ever-loving heck out of Van, oh yes, she was.

Being one of the ghosts meant she wouldn't have firepower on her side, but she was counting on the fact she'd still have speed and—despite the limited visibility and range of motion her Slimer costume afforded her—agility.

When Van blasted the horn on her megaphone, Willa ran for the table full of harnesses and satchels. Slinging the harness over her shoulders and clipping it in the middle, she had to laugh. The thing barely fit around Slimer's lumps. How in the hell was she going to haul the satchel around? She'd counted on being able to sling it messenger-bag style over a shoulder, but it wasn't going to fit over her ginormous green head.

Then there was someone at her side, tugging her hand. "Try this one."

Van handed her a different satchel, this one with an adjustable strap, and then helped her work it over her head. Perfect.

"You know I'm not going to take pity on you out there." There was laughter in Van's voice, and it did something to Willa's insides. Made them all toasty warm. She wanted to hear that tone of voice again—maybe when they were naked in the cabin, because surely that's how this was going to end up?

"I'm not going to show you any mercy either. I hope you made sure the slime was washable, because I'd hate to ruin your coveralls."

Jesus, coveralls had no right sounding sexy. Three months ago, she would've vociferously denied they could ever be. But Van... All Willa could think about was how she wanted to uncover all the things that damn jumpsuit was hiding.

"This ain't my first rodeo." Van had already picked up one of the proton packs and took the opportunity to pose with her gun before sliding her goggles over her eyes.

"May the best—" Willa's sporting good wishes were cut off by another blast of the megaphone's buzzer, and that was the cue to scatter.

———

VAN WATCHED Willa take off into the woods, dyed tennis skirt swinging in an incredibly tempting way high up on those muscular thighs of hers. She was slowed some by the satchel wedged over her shoulder and her Slimer get-up, but she could still outrun everyone else.

If she wanted to get a shot in, Van would have to rely on stealth, because she sure as hell wasn't going to outrun Willa. Even with that damn papier-mâché thing restricting her move ments, she wouldn't expect Willa to be clumsy. Which was proven by the fact that Willa had just vaulted over a fallen log like a post-nuclear apocalypse gazelle.

Van's hands itched to pump the gun, but the old-school video game pistol didn't have any moving parts, so she'd have to fake it and make some convincing sound effects.

She followed Willa at a walk, keeping an eye out for ghosts who would take her out with a slime ball or paint pellets, aiming for their targets when she had a shot. She passed by two campers before reaching the border of the woods Willa had sprinted toward and gingerly climbing over the fallen log Willa had so easily leapt over. Partly because she didn't trust her own two feet not to trip her up, but also there was no way in hell she was going to do anything to put her equipment at risk. She and Nate had busted their asses on these things.

Van stalked through the trees, trying to stay alert for any crunch of leaves or snapping of twigs that might mean someone was nearby. But all she could hear were distant shouts of both victory and agony. If nothing else, people were having fun, and she'd helped make that happen. It was a good feeling.

———

WILLA RAN AS FAR and as fast as she could until her lungs started to hurt, confident there was no freaking way Van would be able to keep up. Girl might be a goddamn genius, but in shape, she was not. Which was good, because Willa needed some advantage in this competition.

She could lurk around the outer borders of the field of play that had been established until things quieted down some, but that seemed unsporting. Also it wasn't in her nature to sit still. Her fingers itched with the adrenaline of competition, and all she wanted to do was slime someone, watch that gooey green stuff Van had whipped up drip down someone's clothes.

Heart racing, she stalked along the border, listening for any close-by sounds, but only hearing distant shouts. Sure sounded like people were having a good time. She hoped wherever Van was that she could hear them too. She'd have to remember to call Nate and tell him as well—it was a major bummer he'd had to miss this, but then again Willa couldn't be too sorry because Nate's idiotic injury had meant she'd finally gotten a shot with Van, a shot she wasn't going to blow. If she played her cards right, this had potential. And not just for a semester of dirty texts and sexy snapchats, but…more.

A crunch of a branch behind her activated Willa's reflexes. She swung around to face the direction the noise had come from, dropped to her knees, grabbed a slimeball out of her satchel, and threw when she caught a glimpse of a taupe jumpsuit. But the only color Willa cared about was the satisfying bright green splatter that resulted when her ball hit the mark and exploded as someone shouted.

After she'd caught her breath, she took a second to figure out who her victim was and came face to…well, papier-mâché Slimer costume with none other than Michael Tully.

"You're not going to fire me for sliming you, right?"

Michael shook his head, and Willa enjoyed the way the slime dripped from his coveralls and onto the ground. Fully biodegradable, Van had assured her. Well, right after she'd mumbled something about Willa having higher standards than the EPA.

"No, but you might have to answer to Heather. She was looking forward to sliming me herself, and now you've deprived her of the pleasure."

Oops. Well, Heather would have to beat Michael at something else. She'd been surprisingly good as a light saber gladiator the other night.

"Sorry, not sorry. Now head back to the boathouse. I've got more slimeballs to throw."

Michael loped off in the direction of camp, and Willa continued on her trek, busting a few more Ghostbusters she happened upon who were trying to hide behind a bank of trees. Even though she knew she shouldn't because it would attract attention, she had to let out a cry of "Busted, suckers!"

Yeah, Heather probably wouldn't appreciate her yelling at guests, but she couldn't fault Willa for getting so into the spirit of the game. That's what she was always after them to do, right?

———

Bless Willa's complete and utter lack of ability to stay silent in the face of victory. The cry of "Busted, suckers!" made Van's head whip around. She'd calmly walked toward where Willa had disappeared into the woods, keeping her Duck Hunt gun primed at her chest. While she'd been keeping an eye out for other players who could take her out, she hadn't been trying to score kills.

After all, there were two ways to win this game, and she was only interested in one of them: having Willa at her disposal for the rest of the night. Even if that hadn't been her goal, her strategy would have been the same. When you were smart but lazy and out of shape—not that she'd ever been *in* shape—it made more sense to let the other, more enthusiastic players take each other out. Then even the survivors would be exhausted. Of course, this whole thing fell apart if everyone had the same attitude.

Fortunately, she knew Willa couldn't help herself from going full steam ahead when there was a competition in front of her. Also lucky for Van, Willa was rather vocal in her triumphs. Willa's exuberant shout echoed through her ears, and she headed toward where the war cry had come from. On her way, she managed to take out a few ghosts who were practically lounging by a tree and didn't seem all that upset to be knocked out of the game.

Unlike the agonized cries in response to a euphoric yell of "You got slimed, marshmallow man!"

Willa must've busted the guy Van had seen earlier in a pretty realistic Stay Puft costume. Van hoped the slime she'd cooked up would wash out of that fabric...

She didn't have time to fret over that detail, though, because she had a Slimer to track. Whatever benevolent god created Holtzmann must have been with her because the marshmallow dude was not going gently into the good night. Oh no, he was raging. Had maybe had one too many drinks at dinner. Either that or he was getting into this way more than was strictly necessary. Whatever the case, the racket he continued to create made it easy to both find him and sneak up on him, lest Willa still be there.

But the green goblin had fled already, and all that was left was a half-deflated Stay Puft with a pathetically sagging cap on his head. After Van had determined they were, in fact, alone, she snuck over to the still-wailing dude.

"Hey," she said in a hushed voice. "I'm gunning for that Slimer who took you out. Which way'd she go?"

Like the vengeful soul he was, he raised one puffy arm to point toward camp.

Van took off at a jog, which was pretty much her maximum speed, and soon enough there were more noises and disgruntled 'busters and ghosts alike that Willa had left in her wake. Not a one of them refused when Van asked which way Slimer had gone.

About an hour after the game had started, she'd come nearly full-circle back to camp, and given her calculations, she and Willa were probably some of the last players still standing. Not that

Van cared about winning the whole shebang. No, she'd let anyone slime the heck out of her or stand still as one of Willa's beloved rocks to allow another Ghostbuster to zap her if they let her down Slimer first. There was no staff member she wanted to slime worse than she wanted to have Willa at her mercy tonight.

Another victory cry went up. "Boo-yah! I outclassed your ass, class four apparition!"

So Willa *had* paid attention when they were watching and was coming up with personally crafted taunts for everyone she busted. That was… Van rolled her shoulders and shimmied in her jumpsuit, because that was kinda hot is what it was.

Then Van saw her, standing over her latest "kill." From the back, it was everything she could've asked for in a woman: super-fly cosplay and a damn fine ass. The ingenuity of cutting a hole out of the back of Slimer's head to let her blonde ponytail swing free was as effective at jumpstarting Van's libido as any aphrodisiac, maybe more.

While Willa was still celebrating her victory, Van took up position behind a tree on one knee to steady her shot and confuse her target. She was only going to have one chance to zap Willa, or the much more athletic woman would have her slimed beyond belief within seconds.

So she took a deep breath, muttered a prayer to Holtzmann, and then called Willa's name.

Slimer whipped around, and it was almost comical the way the green papier-mâché gremlin seemed to search for where the noise had come from. By the time Willa/Slimer had located her, it was too late. Van had her dead to rights, pulling her trigger and setting the tag off, the screen blinking a satisfying slime green and a cry rising up from the beast as though she'd mortally wounded it instead of merely triggering the electro-luminescent backlight of the tag.

Victory was sweet indeed.

14

THEY BARELY MADE it back to the cabin before they were kicking their shoes off. Willa couldn't wait to get her stupid Slimer costume off. It was surprisingly hot—probably because papier-mâché wasn't exactly breathable—and plus it was starting to chafe under her arms, which was unpleasant.

Her competitive pride was somewhat bruised by her loss, but excitement was curling low in her belly. Van had bested her, which meant, until the sun came up, she was Van's to do with what she pleased. Which was at once unnerving and also ridiculously sexy. She'd never been much for the bedroom games she heard other people talk about. While she'd like to claim it wasn't the result of her being a control freak, on some level that was it. She'd never found someone who she trusted enough to hand over any sort of control. But Van...

The door to the cabin slammed closed, and then there were hands tugging at the bottom of her Slimer suit. Willa raised her arms to help aid in the stripping and was momentarily plunged into darkness as Van lifted the thing off of her.

"Ugh, is the fire for the s'mores still going? Because I want to burn this thing."

When she could see again, she was confronted by Van's outraged face. "You will do no such thing. If you aren't keeping him, I'm going to."

"And where, pray tell, are you going to keep it?"

Van's scowl deepened, and Willa had to smother a smile. "Don't call Slimer 'it.' Show some respect, for god's sake. I'm going to put him…"

Van held Slimer up in the corner of the cabin, probably planning exactly how to suspend the thing—sorry, *him*—in midair, and if she was unlucky, how to make him fly around and terrorize her. Had it been anyone else, she would've been irritated, but she just found Van so goddamn charming. "Here."

Yep, there was that smile Willa couldn't—and to be honest, didn't want to—fight against. She set indignant hands on her hips and cocked them, making her skirt ride up on one side. "Fine, but how about you work out your suspension system tomorrow? Unless you want to make use of your night of free rein by employing me as your lab assistant."

Infuriating woman actually seemed to consider it, but then tossed Slimer onto a pile of laundry, facedown. Good. She didn't want Slimer seeing what would come next.

"No. I've got plans for you."

Van's dark eyes raked over her, and though there obviously wasn't any physical contact, her skin prickled and tingled as if there were. She could imagine Van's blunt fingers—still stained with her last-ditch efforts to finish up her project—trailing over and over her body. Ached for it, actually.

Willa had to hold herself back as Van walked toward her, intent bright in Van's eyes. Those fingers Willa longed for instead took hold of the flap on Van's coveralls and pulled, the sound of unsnapping going straight to her core. Another snap followed and another, until the gap reached Van's waist. She shrugged the top off to reveal a skintight ribbed undershirt, and Willa's mouth watered.

Van tied the loose sleeves at her waist and then set her own hands on her hips, and Willa couldn't help but stare. The lighting in the cabin was less than ideal, but she could still see Van's nipples through the thin, white fabric. God love the woman for rarely wearing a bra. Willa wanted to sink to her knees, wrap her arms around Van's waist, and take one of those hard points into her mouth to suckle without even bothering to push the shirt out of her way.

Van was the one who'd won their bet, though, and now it was time to pay the piper. Or the 'buster as the case may be. And her 'buster was looking intent on payment indeed.

Van lifted her small pointy chin. "Skirt off."

"But you—"

"Yes, I love your skirt, and I'd like it even better on the floor. Strip, Willa."

How many teenage nights had Willa spent hearing those words while she furtively touched herself under her covers? The wetness gathered between her thighs like it had on those nights in the dark, but now it wouldn't be her own fingers stroking that intimate flesh. A shiver ran through her just thinking about it, which seemed perfectly reasonable when one of her deepest-held fantasies was coming true.

So she reached for the hook at the side of her skirt and undid it, grabbing the zipper and sliding it down until she could shimmy out of the pleated fabric.

"Shorts too."

Right. She'd slipped on some ass-hugging Spandex things, the shortest ones she had because she'd wanted to flash Van a little cheek as Willa left her in the dust. Willa worked them down her thighs, Van's gaze zooming in on her underwear right away, and Willa could swear there was a quiet curse word in response.

Yes, she'd thought Van would like these. She'd maybe worn them on purpose. Baby pink and lacy, they showed off more than they covered up.

"Shirt."

Willa obliged, stripping her own tank over her head and discarding it on the floor.

"Hair down."

Wow, she must've done something right, because rarely was Van so monosyllabic when they were together like this. In the past two-plus weeks of sexytimes, sometimes it had even been necessary for Willa to put a finger over her delicious mouth to hush the running commentary so they could kiss. Not now. Now she'd stolen the words out of Van's mouth and left her with only the briefest of instructions.

Willa tugged the elastic out of her hair and shook it out so it fell below her shoulders. It was amazing how good Van could make her feel without even laying a finger on her—the way Van looked at her could make her sturdy knees weak.

Then she and Van were toe-to-toe, and Willa had to look slightly down to keep eye contact. Van took another step forward, and Willa had to bite off the groan rising in her throat as the knot Van had fashioned from her discarded sleeves pressed against Willa's pelvis, as if more attention needed to be drawn there. Instead, Willa's teeth sunk into her lip and she closed her eyes.

"That's a good idea," Van muttered, almost to herself. "Keep your eyes closed."

Oh jeez. Willa's body tensed, but she did as she'd been told, never one to renege on a promise. That's when Van touched her, and she sucked a breath into her lungs as Van ran a finger from her navel up to the band of her sports bra. It was the only front-closure one she had, and she was glad she'd worn it tonight.

Van toyed with the zipper at the front of her chest, and Willa couldn't help but shift. Was this what she was in for? A long night of being teased? She didn't think she could take it.

Van didn't seem to have bottomless wells of patience either, tugging at the zipper until it came undone and then pushing the straps off Willa's shoulders. Now she was mostly naked in front of Van. Which shouldn't have been disconcerting, given they'd been entirely naked together before, but this was different somehow. Maybe because the lights were on and she was standing here like a mannequin in a lingerie shop? Or maybe because this was the first time she'd been with a partner and started having images of a future together flit through her brain regularly.

It was a heady combination of nerves and excitement, picturing going out on an actual date with Van, having her visit and picking her up at the airport with nothing more than a backpack because she'd have a drawer at Willa's place.

Whatever it was, it made her breath come shallow and fast, made her clench her hands into fists as Van set warm hands under her breasts. *Touch me.* Was she not supposed to make demands? The rules of this bet hadn't specified.

"Van, please."

"Please what?"

The callused pads of Van's thumbs traced the bottom-most curve of her breasts, sliding first out to the side of her ribs, nearly to her armpits, and then back to where they would meet in the center.

"Touch me please."

"I am touching you."

Infuriating woman. "More. I want you to touch me more."

Then the maddening hands were drifting down her ribcage, her stomach, fingers and thumbs forming a W that drifted down to her waist and stayed there. Then Van was toying with the waistband of her underwear, thumbs skimming along the top of the lace, sometimes dipping underneath. Willa shivered, her skin prickling with goosebumps. This was not what she'd had in mind.

Van coasted her hands back up, and there was the most welcome sensation in the world of her breasts being hefted, weighed in Van's hands. She'd sometimes cursed her chest—large breasts weren't particularly helpful in athletics and could be a downright pain in the ass. Well, more like back and shoulders. With Van's hands on her, though, she felt beautiful and wanted. Even with her eyes closed, she could feel Van's desire pouring off her in waves.

Van toyed with her for a while, squeezing gently and running thumbs over her rapidly hardening nipples, all while moisture gathered between her legs, probably soaking what little fabric was there. When she was about to plead again, Van dropped her breasts, and she made a small noise at the sudden weight. It didn't hurt precisely. In fact, it made the string of desire running between her breasts and her pussy pull tight. Hell.

"You're going to lie on your bed." Willa opened her mouth to protest, because she couldn't see a damn thing and there was no way she was going to try to navigate the minefield that was their cabin floor. Like as not, she'd probably step on a Lego. "Don't worry, I'll take you."

One hand about Willa's waist and another in her hand, Van steered Willa toward her bed, and when Willa felt the cotton of her duvet at the backs of her knees, she sat. Van cradled the back of her head and helped her lie down. It was strangely thrilling, the careful way Van was handling her, and it continued to thrill her as Van steered Willa's hands to the top of the bed where she wrapped Willa's fingers around the metal rung there.

"Don't let go, no matter what I do."

What in heaven's name did the woman propose to do? There was some shuffling that made Willa uneasy, but she breathed through it, much as she would a point in a big match. In some ways, there was less at stake here—there was no one she'd let down—but also so much more. This thing she had with Van...it didn't feel temporary and it didn't feel casual. And Van herself... she seemed different somehow too.

Maybe it was that they were both adults now, but behind that charming and zany—and yes, sometimes grumpy—exterior, she'd discovered a gentle and thoughtful person, someone who she thought about a lot. While some of the hero worship was still there, which was part of what made this so goddamn exciting, she also felt like she had something to offer Van. She wasn't a kid anymore.

While she'd been meditating on their relationship, Van had apparently found what she'd been looking for in the swamp she called her side of the room. The side of the narrow bed sank, and while Willa wanted so desperately to open her eyes, she wouldn't. A good thing too, because a second later, something soft and stretchy was slipping over her closed eyes.

"What—"

"It's my Wonder Woman sweatband."

If one of Willa's teammates or country club friends had said that, she'd be grossed out. She didn't want someone else's sweat-drenched athletic gear all over her face. But she knew Van—she wasn't the working out type. Also there was no way she'd sully anything with her beloved Wonder Woman's symbol on it, even if it were a thing built specifically to be soiled.

"Why are you smiling?"

"Because I know you."

There was a shift of the mattress, and before she could even take a breath, Van was straddling her and then kissing her. God did that woman know how to kiss. Which was a little surprising. Van had made it sound like she spent more time with her books than with actual people—and even less with people of the romantically involved sort—but you'd never know it from what she could do with her mouth.

As quickly as the kiss had started, it was over, and Willa was left craning her neck for more. What she got was an open-mouthed kiss with a whisper of a lick on the side of her neck, just under her ear, and then another right where her jaw started to curve. Van sucked at her skin, and though she wouldn't have thought so before now, that small act made her squirm under-neath Van's weight. Made her want Van to mouth every last part of her. Especially when Van finished off with a nip and moved lower. Teeth skimming along Willa's collarbone, kisses being dropped between her breasts, until Van's tongue circled her navel.

It was a good thing Van was straddling her, otherwise, she surely would've squirmed off the bed by now. As it was, Van tutted at her.

"How…"

A bite caught the edge of her bellybutton.

"Am I…"

A kiss dropped on one of her hipbones.

"Supposed…"

A lick and a long suck to the rise on the other side of her pelvis. Willa hoped Van would leave a bruise—to show that Van had seen fit to mark her, claim her, that Van delighted in the taste of her skin that much. The thought made her internal muscles clench in a wish for penetration.

"To torture you…"

Van slid back, moving her straddle from Willa's hips to her shins, and kissed right above the line of Willa's scant underwear.

"If you don't…"

Then Van's weight was gone, soon replaced by her hands spreading Willa's knees to make room for her. Followed by fingers hooking into the sides of her underwear, more fingers urging her to lift her hips, and then the barely there lace was sliding down her legs until it was gone altogether.

"Stay..."

Van's weight shifted again and though Willa was tempted to release her hands, rip the makeshift blindfold from her eyes, and dig her fingers into Van's hair, she contented herself with a whimper. Van was going to kill her. She was going to die from desire in this cabin, and there would be inquiries, and what kind of reputation would that give Camp Firefly Falls? The poor Tullys.

Then there was a warm breath between her legs, and Willa started chanting in her head. *Yes, please. Come on, Van, please.*

"Still?"

Then Van's thumbs were parting her labia, spreading her out so Van could have access and use that ridiculously gifted mouth of hers precisely where Willa wanted it. A broad lick right over her clit sent shudders through her entire body and a groan from her mouth.

Not that she would wish for it, but the teasing had her so sensitive, so ready to blow, she wasn't sure why precisely she wasn't coming all over Van's face right this second. God she was close, but that blunt contact was only enough to make her crazy, not quite what she needed to go off.

Van repositioned a hand, and then her fingers were sliding inside of Willa, first two and then three, followed quickly by suction and the flick of Van's tongue over the center of Willa's pleasure.

That. That was what she needed to get off. She gripped the bar above her head so hard she wouldn't have been surprised if it came off in her hands, and her hips pressed up, needing the contact of Van's mouth against her core, needing the push and spread of Van's fingers inside her.

Her climax seemed to go on forever, like tiny aftershocks

from an earthquake, skillfully drawn out by Van, until she couldn't stand being touched anymore. It was too much to bear, and her head was so scrambled she could barely find the words.

"Done, Van, done. Can't. No more."

There was a soft chuckle from beyond the blindfold, and with one last kiss pressed just above the line of her pubic hair, Van slid out her fingers and moved from between Willa's legs. Willa pressed her knees together, needing to feel closed off after being blown wide open. She only realized she was still clutching the bar when Van gently pried her fingers from around it. They were stiff and sore, unenthusiastic about being straightened out after being violently curled for so long. Van was tender, taking her time easing the kinks out, kissing Willa's knuckles, sucking lightly on her fingertips.

If Willa hadn't been left boneless by that earth-shattering orgasm, Van's soothing attentions would've rendered her so. Even when Van slid the blindfold up to her hairline, she didn't open her eyes, but stayed in the dreamy half-dark behind her eyelids.

"'Mazing. Anyone ever tell you you're a fucking genius?"

A huffed laugh as Van stretched out beside her and nestled under one of Willa's arms to rest her head on Willa's chest. "Well, sure, but it's usually in a professional context, not actual fucking."

"Morons."

More laughter, but Willa didn't care. If Van could make her come like that, she could laugh at her however much she wanted.

Willa had every intention of reciprocating—or at least having manners enough to *offer* to reciprocate—but before she could, she fell asleep.

———

VAN'S DREAMS had always been places where wishes came true.

Some people had nightmares, but she never had. Dreams were always vivid fulfillment of her every desire.

She'd thought about nudging Willa awake from where she'd basically passed out—girl was a stickler for hygiene and Van couldn't imagine she'd be pleased to wake with un-brushed teeth —but she couldn't bring herself to do it. She'd snuck out of the narrow bed herself to do her night routine and get out of her coveralls and into some flannel pajama pants so old they were verging on threadbare.

Standing in the middle of the cabin, she debated: to climb back alongside Willa or go to her own bed? Aside from being super-awesome at the sexing, they hadn't established what was going on with them. Dating? If so, what would Nate say? The thought made her stomach curdle.

Plus, in less than a week, they'd be packing up the cabin and Willa would be heading back to Stanford, and Van would be back in Charlottesville, dreading the immersion of getting back into the swing of academic life.

If this was just a summer fling—and what the hell else could it possibly be given the circumstances?—she'd glean every moment of pleasure she could out of this week, like sucking marrow from picked-clean bones. Back to lay beside Willa it was, and as she settled in, she tried to program her dreams. Perhaps it would work, perhaps not, but it was so worth a try.

She fell asleep to visions of kissing Willa, and yeah, Willa getting braver in her exploration of Van's body. It was sweet she was tentative, making Van aware that, though she was no Lady Casanova, she'd still had more experience with women than Willa had. What she wouldn't give for Willa to be as aggressive in bed as she was on the court, though.

It turned out Van didn't need to wait for her subconscious to provide. What felt like only minutes after she'd fallen asleep, Willa's husky voice was hot in her ear.

"Van?"

"Yeah?"

"Are you awake?"

"No."

There was a beat of silence and then an elbow to her ribs that made her laugh.

"You are so."

"Yes, I am. What's up?"

Please don't say, "Could you get out of my bed now that you made me come so hard pinecones rolled off the roof?"

She didn't.

She didn't, in fact, say anything at all. Instead of forming words or sounds, Willa used her perfectly lush lips to kiss below Van's ear before taking the lobe between her teeth, softly at first and then harder, with a tug.

In the name of everything Holtzmann...

The tug seemed to head straight for Van's breasts, making them feel hot and needy, nipples hard and ready to be fondled or sucked. What Van wouldn't give to have Willa do to her nipples what she was doing to her goddamn earlobe. Not to mention there was a slight pulse in her core that sent want through every inch of her body.

These feelings could, of course, be explained by chemical reactions, which were sexy in their own way. Van thought, at least. She'd like to get to know Willa better before she attempted to seduce her by murmuring science-nothings in her ear though, describing everything in terms of the nuts and bolts of the human body and not some magical process of divine arousal.

Though, by this point, Willa's mouth had begun to travel lower, and divine was absolutely the word for how it felt to have that woman touching her this way. Willa's fingers rested on Van's stomach, scratching lightly with nails through the worn ribbed cotton of Van's shirt. It would've tickled if it hadn't simply enhanced the feeling that endorphins and hormones were coursing through her system at an unprecedented rate. Along with her heartbeat and her blood, hot with lust, pumping through her veins.

Van was pretty sure it wasn't possible to die of horniness, but if these few minutes had been any indication, she could come damn close.

"Please, please be doing what I think you're doing." If she were a dude, her voice would've cracked. As things were, it came out a croak.

"What do you think I'm doing?"

In the dark, Van could barely see the outline of Willa's head, backlit by the faint glow of the moon and stars from outside.

"Exacting your revenge?"

"If by exacting my revenge, you mean hoping to give you an orgasm half as good as the one you gave me earlier, then yes. That is precisely what I'm doing."

Van's eyes rolled back in her head. She wished she had little Willa Carter on tape saying orgasm. No, she didn't. Nate would no doubt find it, and she'd find him rocking in a corner with his ears plugged, humming the Imperial Death March. Nah, Nate might look like he was being strangled by the Force, but only for a few seconds. He was reasonably cool as big brothers went, at least about the sex part. No paternalistic, prudish attitudes in Nate Carter's head—at least that he would cop to—and Van would happily take credit for some of that. What he probably wouldn't take kindly to is Van hurting Willa in any way.

Willa's hot mouth closed over one of Van's nipples and subjected it to the same treatment as her earlobe. Including the scrape of teeth. That's when all thoughts of the other Carter went entirely out the window.

"Ah!"

As soon as the delectable motion had begun, it stopped, and

Van slammed her head back into the pillow. *Don't stop, don't stop, please don't stop.*

"Did I hurt you? Am I doing this wrong? Is it—"

Van shook her head, hoping Willa could see the movement in the dark. "No, that felt amazing. Really, really amazing. The only way it could be better is if—"

Her instruction was cut off by Willa tugging at the neck of her tank, pulling it down beneath her breast, and starting over, this time with no cotton between the sensitive peak and Willa's sinful mouth. The way she moved her tongue and sucked hard... Van dropped her head back again, and this time made an effort to make her noise less ambiguous.

"Fuck, Willa, I love it when you do that." Willa's hand had joined the fun, cupping and squeezing the part of Van's breast that wasn't in her mouth. Van's back arched off the bed with the added stimulation, and she moaned again.

"You're going to wake up the neighbors, you know."

Pfft. As if they'd be the first cabin to be a-rockin' at Camp Firefly Falls. Rumor had it this place had almost ruined, but then saved Heather and Michael's marriage. Maybe their falling in love again was a good luck charm, because there sure had been a lot of people who found their happy endings—or really, beginnings—here. But she had a better idea than telling Willa about her ridiculous woowoo ideas.

"How about you shut me up, then?"

Of course, her competitive Amazon took the bait and raised her mouth to slant against Van's, silencing her. Van couldn't help but thread her fingers through Willa's hair. In the dark, it looked more silver than gold, but it was so silky her hands passed right through it without meaning to. On the next pass, she knew better and wound it around her fingers to hold Willa fast against her, their lips meeting, parting, and their tongues caressing each other.

They were lying side by side now, and Van took advantage to hook a leg over Willa's hip. Not only did Willa not resist, she grabbed Van's ass and pulled her closer, until their breasts were pushing together and goddamn if that wasn't one of the sexiest feelings in the world.

Their limbs and tongues tangled all up together, and it was getting difficult to tell who ended and started where. Then Willa hitched Van's leg even higher, bringing Willa's thigh between Van's legs in such a way that made her groan into Willa's mouth. Van rocked her hips, creating friction and pressure against her clit, and Willa tightened her grip on Van's ass and urged her forward again. "Does that feel good?"

Van buried her head against Willa's shoulder, hiding out in that curtain of cornsilk hair. "Yeah, it feels good."

"I like it too. I like how you feel, rubbing on me. Do you think you could come from this?"

Van had to laugh, a short half-snort. "I don't think—I know."

"Then do it, Van. I want to feel you come on me. I want to hold you while you come."

Who was she to say no to that? So she rocked her hips again, the pressure and the rasping contact exquisite. Bonus, it left their hands and mouths free to touch everywhere, kiss everywhere. Then the tension had ratcheted as high as it could go, and the string of her desire snapped. Maybe not as intense as climaxes she'd had from fingers or oral, but the shallower waves seemed to roll out for longer, and she relished every last pulse as she rocked out on Willa's bare muscular thigh.

Their foreheads touched as Van panted, clutching Willa for all she was worth. "Revenge exacted."

Willa laughed, that throaty rasping thing, and then laid a kiss on Van's forehead that made her glow inside. That wasn't something you did to a fuck buddy—that was genuine affection, as was the way Willa held her and stroked her back as she drifted off

And genuine affection, that was the kind of thing that should have set off flares in Van's brain.

This thing with Willa wasn't about intimacy; it was about sex and fun and eighties nostalgia. It wasn't about holding hands and...and sleeping together face-to-face. So yeah, there was a ping of terror at the back of her head about what was going on here, but the far, far bigger problem was that it was only a ping. Should've been a symphony, a cacophony of noisy-ass shit going off in her head. But as hard as she looked for it, it wasn't there. What was there was a happy little warm fuzzy who was super-excited about the idea of having Willa Carter in her bed and in her life not just for the next few days, but for the foreseeable future. She was completely and utterly fucked.

15

WILLA NEVER CHECKED her phone during lessons, but she did occasionally take advantage of the passing time between sessions to take a peek. Not that there had been all that much to look forward to. An occasional email from her parents, sometimes a stupid forward from Nate. No, mostly what she got was mail from the university, and that had slowed to a trickle over the summer after the first flurry of communications about the damn cave collapsing.

It was picking back up, though, as the beginning of the school year got closer—class announcements, department meetings, and always something from the bursar. There was something, though, that caught her attention amongst the standard academic minutiae. With a headline of GOOD NEWS, it could only be meant to

Of course she clicked on that first and found a message from her advisor.

WILLA,

I'm thrilled to inform you Hendecasyll Cave has been cleared, and our equipment retrieved. In even better news, the damage was not c

bad as we had feared, and we'll be able to have access again next summer. In the best news of all, the small quake that closed our section of the cave also had the effect of creating a fissure toward the back of our site, and it appears as though there's another cave connecting, which by rough estimates looks twice as large as our original site and with multiple shield formations.

THE REST of the email prattled on about how the safety of the new cave would need to be examined, but it was likely that she and another graduate student would have access to that site next summer as well.

A site no human eyes had laid eyes on maybe ever? Or, at least, never recorded? She'd dreamed about this as a kid, although her focus then had been more on finding long-buried treasures and not so much speleothems. While she'd sure as hell take gold and jewels if there were some, she'd happily settle for new formations to study and catalogue.

Her adventurer's heart sang, and she had to practically tear the phone from her own fingers to wrestle it back into her bag to keep from reading the email a fourth time after her next student had shown up. This was going to be amazing, and she couldn't wait to tell Van. On her way, she'd tell Nate. She'd been meaning to get in touch with him anyway, but had had her hands full...of Van.

As usual, Nate didn't wait for her to announce herself.

"Hey, Willa Nilla."

"What's up, Nate the Great?"

"I think I've gained twenty pounds from Mom's cooking."

"I'm betting it's more from the Tipsy Arnies."

"That's what I said, Mom's cooking."

Willa snorted. Her mother's lack of skill in the kitchen was a family joke, although since they'd become adults her expertise at the wet bar had more than made up for it. In the meantime, their dad had been in charge of feeding the kids.

"So to what do I owe the pleasure of this call? You've been neglecting me."

"I've been…busy."

"Oh, yeah? With who?"

"What is that supposed to mean?"

"Whenever you start seeing someone, you drop off the face of the Earth. Even when you've got finals, I still get more texts than when you've got a new love interest."

She'd like to be able to protest, but couldn't. It wasn't one of her more admirable habits, but as things went, it wasn't the worst she could do.

"Well, what I actually called you about was that my cave, Hendecasyll, is going to be open next summer. It looks like it's bigger than they thought, and if it's safe, I'll have an even bigger cavern to do my fieldwork in. How cool is that?"

"That's awesome. See? I knew it would all work out. And in the meantime, you got to spend a month and a half at camp. Best of all worlds. Also, you should know I got an email from Heather yesterday. She said you're doing a great job, and she was wondering if she would be able to get one of us back next summer. I haven't written her back because I wasn't sure of either of our plans, but I thought you'd like to know that, if she could have you, she'd want you."

That did make Willa happy. She wouldn't be able to come back because hopefully she'd be crawling around in a cavern with a headlamp strapped to her forehead, taking pictures and samples and mapping the place, but it was nice to be wanted.

"That's so nice. I love Heather. I'm glad I could help out."

"All right, your cave was the real reason you called, but what's your excuse for *not* having called? What's his name? Her name? Do I need to break out the shotgun?"

"We don't have a shotgun, and you know as well as I do you're a total pushover when it comes to the people I date. You act all hardass with me, and then you end up playing video games with them and being more upset than I am when we break up."

All of that was true, which Willa appreciated. Not the aftermath of breakups, because it was like taking a shiny new toy away from a child, but the rest of it was nice.

"You're avoiding the question."

"Ugh, fine. But you need to be chill about this, okay?"

"My middle name is chill."

"You don't have a middle name."

"Whatever. Spill the beans, Wills."

She took a deep breath and looked up into the sky. Perfect weather—there were only a few puffy white clouds dotting the canvas of blue. Hopefully telling Nate about her and Van wouldn't be some kind of curse. Everything was going so well, and she really didn't want Nate to rain on her parade.

"I've been…hooking up. With Van."

———

ONE OF THE great pleasures of camp life as far as Van was concerned was being able to make it to the dining hall before Willa did. She could sit at their usual table with an eye on the main entrance and wait for her pretty…Willa. They didn't have to have a word for what was going on. And if they did have to label it, Van wouldn't be sure what to call it.

Even not knowing was providing Van with some relief. If she was fretting about how exactly her relationship with Willa was defined, then she wasn't giving herself a stomachache thinking about having to go back to the university in a week.

Dread was not a strong enough word for what she felt about having to go back to that campus. Here it was easy enough to keep that life in a box—deal with the emails that came along and then get back to what Heather was paying her for. Once she left Camp Firefly Falls and was back in Charlottesville in her crappy apartment with the weight of her profession pressing down on her relentlessly…

So much for not giving herself a stomachache. Dinner had looked good too, though she'd been waiting for Willa before she picked any up.

Would Willa have had time to run back to their cabin to shower before coming to dinner? As shallow as it made her, she hoped not. She liked the way Willa's blonde wisps framed her pinked-up face after she'd been hard-charging all over the court. Those sexy-ass tennis skirts didn't hurt either. Except she'd left in that drop-waist dress with the pleats on the bottom this morning. That particular shape didn't do anything for Willa's chest, but damn did it show off her long, strong limbs.

As a bonus, it was fewer items of clothing to take off her when they got back to the cabin. Another perk of camp life—sharing a cabin and therefore a bathroom with one's…lover? God how she loved to soap Willa up and rinse her off before getting her naked and warm in one of their beds. Van's mind had already started to wander with thoughts of what they'd enjoy for their carnal dessert when someone sat down across the table from her.

The woman was vaguely familiar, but that didn't give Van any hints—that's what most people at camp looked like to her, aside from Willa, Michael, Heather, and a few other people she interacted with regularly. So was this black woman staff or a camper? Hopefully she'd say and not force Van to embarrass herself.

"Van, I'm so sorry to interrupt your evening. I'll make this quick. My name is Michelle Brown, and I'm one of the team leaders with Aquitaine. We've been having a great time here this week, and my favorite was the laser tag. Admittedly, I go knocked out by a rampaging Slimer pretty quickly, but it was fun and my team loved it."

Heather thanked her regularly, but it was always nice to hear positive feedback, especially about something that had been her baby. "Thanks for telling me. I had fun putting it together."

Michelle smiled and looked at Van closely, eyes narrowed slightly. "This might sound stalker-ish, but I didn't assemble the top-producing team at Aquitaine by being a shrinking violet. I looked up your CV. I saw you're at UVA. I was wondering if either you had some grad students you might send our way—if they're anywhere near creative as you, I'll take them in a heartbeat—or if I'm very lucky, if you'd ever consider leaving academia?"

Van's mouth fell open, but Michelle went on, holding her hands up. "I know, I know, it's not likely. You've got a tenure-track position at a great school, and people like you have the jobs they want, not the only one they could get. I'm sorry if I seem rude, but I just knew I'd be kicking myself on the flight out if I didn't say anything."

"Well, actually..." Michelle's eyes lit up at those two small words, and Van swore her to secrecy before she continued. After about ten minutes, they wrapped up their conversation with a firm handshake and a promise on Van's part to be in touch if she did, in fact, leave UVA.

Soon after Michelle had rejoined her table in the crowded dining lodge, there was a flash of white at the door, and Willa bounced through.

Either she'd had an especially good lesson or something else noteworthy had happened because the girl looked radiant. Cheeks aglow, mouth wide, and teeth exposed in a smile that was contagious. Then she came toward Van at a jog, took up her hand, and kissed her on the cheek.

Here. In front of everyone.

Heather and Michael had made it clear from the beginning homophobia would not be tolerated. If anyone had a problem with Van, they had a problem with camp and could leave. That promise let Van's heart race with anticipation and delight, but also shock. That kind of stuff was way more "dating" than "hooking up."

They were usually more reserved in front of the campers and the other staff, but Van hadn't been sure if that was an effort to be professional on Willa's part or if PDAs weren't Willa's jam or maybe that since this was just a summer fling, she wanted to keep it on the DL too. But no, it appeared it had been Option A, and Willa was too excited to contain herself. Adorable, yes, but also confusing. Van would worry about it later. "What's up, Wills? Good day?"

"The best." Oh, she was the cutest. Willa grabbed Van's hand and used it to tug Van toward where the food was being served, practically bouncing on her toes. Where did the girl get this much energy? Maybe it was the kale. Eh, Van would stick to caffeine. "I got an email from my advisor, and you'll never guess what she said."

"Get out while you can?"

Willa scowled at Van's joke and shook her head. "No, Debbie Downer. She said we'll be able to get back into Hendecasyll next summer and the quake opened up an undiscovered part of the cavern. So not only do I get to go back to my site, but now there's more of it. Isn't that great?"

Great was not the word Van would use for it. How could Willa not see, after everything Van had shared with her, that academia was not the way to go? Sure, it was fun and sexy now, but in the long run, it would make her miserable. This new cave could be a great opportunity, but it could also be a career-such. What if there was nothing new there? What if they'd seen it all before? What if they were wrong about the safety of it? Or wha if no one gave a shit about a fucking cave and she couldn't get funding?

"Are you sure you're going to get first crack at it?"

Willa's face pulled inward in a frown. "That's what Kathy said. Why would she—"

"Well, if it turns out there's something super-exciting in the new cave, she might call dibs. Then where would you be? Shit out of luck or listed far down on a paper she gets published. You'll end up doing all the work, she'll get all the glory, and when it comes time for you to get a job, all you'll have is a few shitty credits. Honestly, why don't you get your master's and be done with this? You can always go caving as a hobby—what is it, spelunking? You could be a spelunker. And you know, go get a job that will pay for your spelunking habit. Way more fun that way."

Willa's hand slipped out of hers, and when Van turned to see why, Willa had crossed her arms over her chest. "Right."

"Trust me, Wills, it'd be better that way."

Willa didn't reply, but grabbed a plate and started serving herself, jabbing the serving utensils into the food as if it had offended her somehow. Sure, it wasn't easy to hear, but better it should come from Van, who cared about Willa and wanted the best for her, than Willa waking up in six years and realizing she'd wasted so much of her life on a thing she'd grown to despise.

———

AFTER A DINNER and a walk back to the cabin chock full of Van talking about how terrible academic life was, Willa had had enough. "What is your problem?"

Van was being crazy and not in the quirky way Willa loved about her. The absent-mindedness, the distraction when a pot she'd been keeping on the back burner of her mind finally came to a boil and she needed to write it out before her brain bubbled over—those things were endearing. She could even learn to live with the mess—as long as it was contained. This, however, was not okay.

"My problem is that academia is for blowhards who care more about awards and summer vacation than they do for actual science. My problem is I've worked toward this thing my entire life, and now it turns out I'm stuck in a job I hate but it would be stupid to throw it all away and start over. My problem is you're about to make the same mistake I did and I'm trying to warn you, but you won't listen to me. My problem is if I was wrong about this, what else was I wrong about?"

Van's last two points struck Willa square in the chest. She had listened to Van over the past five weeks, had seen how stressed and nuts her job made her. But some of the things Van hated about academia were things Willa loved.

She'd loved being a TA to intro classes, especially because she'd had the chance to take students who were in geology because it was "Rocks for Jocks" and turn them into kids who were genuinely curious. She even enjoyed university politics to some extent. It was like tennis, but in her brain. Strategy, endurance, seeing several steps ahead, approaching your opponent in an elegant but deadly fashion—these were her favorite things about playing the game, and they'd come in handy in her field already.

The begging for funding wasn't exactly fun, but she relished the challenge of writing persuasive grants and she loved her fieldwork.

As for what else Van might be wrong about…what else could she mean but Willa? Did she think the past couple of weeks had been a mistake? Because Willa sure didn't. But if Van thought she was too young and stupid to make good decisions and to know herself… Or maybe she didn't want the competition of another academic. Willa had seen couples who got so competitive with each other they couldn't survive it. Maybe Van wanted little blonde tagalong Willa, Willa who used to fawn all over her and worship the ground she walked on, Willa the skirt-wearing tennis player. If Van wanted her to be a fucking trophy girlfriend, she could take her Holtzmann and shove it.

"Look, Van, I know you're frustrated. I know you're angry and feeling off-kilter, and I'm sorry, okay? I'm sorry being a professor didn't turn out like you wanted and that you feel like you've wasted so much time. It's not too late to get out. You could quit and find something you enjoy. Maybe the private sector would suit you better. Your work could have commercial applications and—"

"Maybe you're okay with quitting, but I'm not."

Ouch. Even though she knew it made her look childish, Willa couldn't help but put her hands on her hips. "I didn't quit tennis. I decided not to pursue going pro, but I played out my four years on the team, and I gave it my best while trying to get good enough grades that I'd be able to get into a reputable graduate program. So don't talk to me about quitting. And you know, if you wanted a dumb jock to fawn all over you and your big brain, you came to the wrong place."

Van shook her head, and her brows pulled together. "I don't want a—"

"Don't you? I see the way you look at me. You like my legs, you like how my ass looks in my skirts. Would you like me as well if I sat in front of a computer or a blackboard all day? I don't think so. Also, you're being a jerk, and you've got your head wedged pretty far up your own ass. Nate told me to take it easy and make sure we were on the same page before I got too wrapped up in you. Clearly I should've done that because the only thing you care about is your own agenda and your own problems."

Van's dark eyes widened, and she looked as panicked as Willa had ever seen her. "You told Nate about us?"

Willa wanted to stomp her foot, but throwing a tantrum wouldn't be okay. It hurt so bad, though, that Van was more upset about Willa telling Nate about their…what she'd thought was a relationship than she was about Willa's feelings. She needed to pound her body against something, and she needed to get out of here.

So Willa found her reasonable, grown-up voice and addressed Van in what she hoped was a calm and rational fashion, swallowing the lump that was forming in her throat. "And that is exactly what I'm talking about. We need to finish this week out for Heather and figure out a way to work together, but I think the sleeping together needs to stop."

What she wanted to say was she didn't want to fool around with Van if she didn't have Van's respect as well as her lust. But saying it out loud would've made it more real, and she didn't want Van to argue anymore. She wanted to get out of here.

"I'm going for a run. I'll see you later."

———

VAN'S BRAIN simmered and stewed in her skull. This was a mess. She was a mess. She'd made a huge mess of things with Willa. It wasn't some silly lovers' spat she could remedy with charm and a screaming orgasm. She'd hurt Willa. Deep down to her core.

Yes, Willa walked around all confident in her preppy clothes and her perfect blonde ponytails, but she had insecurities like anyone else. It was easy to forget because she kept them tucked away and dealt with them so differently from the way Van did, but that didn't mean she didn't have them at all.

It had taken her weeks to figure it out, but that's part of what all her questions about being a professor had been about—Willa not quite believing she had the stuff to make it. Instead of making her feel better or steering clear of Willa's uncertainties, Van had run head first into them. She hadn't meant to, of course, but she'd been so wrapped up in her own misery she hadn't seen how it might make Willa feel.

Not to mention that she'd made it sound like all that mattered were Nate's feelings about them being together and not Willa's. Yeah, she'd freaked, but that wasn't an excuse for letting Willa feel like Van didn't care about her, only her brother.

Now Willa was gone. Technically out for a run, but when she got back, it wouldn't be for fun and games in the shower, it wouldn't be for a movie-fest masquerading as research on Van's bed, and it sure as hell wouldn't be to confide in Van she was worried she wouldn't be able to hack it in her PhD program or score a job once she was done.

They'd be bunkmates and team players to get the job done the last day of Aquitaine's session, help Heather and Michael close up camp, and then Willa would go home to Stanford and Van would go back to another year of misery in Charlottesville. Willa would go back to being Nate's little sister, and when Van dared, she could ask Nate for updates. On the woman she'd fallen flat out in love with. She'd have to hear about Willa's successes—because with every part of her, Van believed Willa would be successful—and not be a part of them. She'd have to hear about her dating someone else, eventually settling down with someone else, maybe having babies with someone else.

That was not going to be okay.

Usually in these circumstances—not that these were usual circumstances because she'd never felt like this about anyone before, but basically when she'd screwed up in a pretty major way —there was only one person she turned to. This was going to be a fucking awkward phone call, but it couldn't possibly be worse than slinking off, knowing she could've fixed things with Willa.

Hell, she hoped she *could* still fix things with Willa, but she'd been a pretty giant nerf-herder. It would mean talking to Nate about being with his sister, but that would be worth it. Watching Willa walk away had torn her up inside, and while she didn't want to lose her friendship with Nate, she couldn't pass up a shot to see if she could have both. Which she very much wanted—all the Carters, all the time. Now she had to woman up and come clean to Nate about having gotten down and dirty with Willa and had come to realize that she wanted oh so much more than that.

She needed something first, though. Digging around in one of her desk drawers, she eventually found what she was looking for. The gold bracelets were dusty from being in there for the whole summer, so she polished them up on her shirt, a few extra swipes on the red stars for good measure, and then slipped them on her wrists. If her Wonder Woman bracelets couldn't help her, nothing could.

16

"Hey, Van Diagram."

If Van's eyes rolled any harder, they were going to fall out of her head. "I cannot even believe you said that. That's the worst pun I've ever heard."

"Yeah, but you like bad puns. And dad jokes. So don't tell me that under that exasperated exterior you're not the least bit amused by me. I mean, come on. Van diagram?"

"Yeah, yeah, all right. That's a good one. You're going to make some child incredibly humiliated someday."

"Always the dream." Yeah, Van could see that. Nate settling down with some girl, having ridiculously adorable babies, and in a few years' time, Nate would have them groaning and covering their eyes in the back of his own damn station wagon. "So what's up, since you clearly weren't calling for my clever jokes?"

Right. That. She could jump right in with both feet into the whole "you know how I've been sleeping with your sister" thing right away, but maybe she should bury that lede. Just for a little while, until her stomach didn't feel so much like it was going to eject its contents.

154 | TAMSEN PARKER

"So you know how I'm the smartest person you know and I always have my shit together?"

She was teasing, but when Nate answered, his tone was all seriousness. "Yeah, I do."

Van didn't know whether to be even more embarrassed than she already was or relieved. Embarrassed because, god, if Nate thought that about her, what she was about to confess might lose his good opinion forever. Relieved because Nate knew her better than anyone else in this world and he wasn't a stupid guy. If he thought that highly of her, he couldn't be completely fucking wrong, right?

"Well, turns out even us know-it-alls don't actually know it all."

"Sure. But in my experience, you can figure out where to find the answer and you can be taught. That's probably more important than knowing everything."

That was definitely true. Those were the students she loved—the ones who said "I don't know" but then did their damnedest to find the answer. Not the ones who merely shrugged and were content to live with their ignorant lot.

"Well, the thing is, I think I hate being a professor."

"I think you do too."

She had been all ready to counter his argument that no, she was just having a rough patch and she should give it longer and surely it would turn out to be everything she'd dreamed of. It took her a second to recalculate. "What the fuck, dude? Were you never going to say anything?"

"What was I supposed to say? 'Hey, Van, this thing you've worked toward your entire life doesn't actually seem to be a good fit. Maybe you should find something else to do.' How many amps of electricity would you have rigged up to shoot through me at the soonest possible opportunity?"

Fair. And the answer was about ten milliamps—enough to really fucking hurt, but not enough to kill him.

"I know better than to try to talk you out of something you've got your mind set on. But you know it's okay to change your mind, right?"

Was it, though? Every time her parents had failed to do something they said they would—when they'd failed to show up at a science fair they'd sworn they would be at, when they'd announced they'd sold their house and were moving to Florida in a week while she'd still been in college—it had sucked. Their constant changing of plans had left her twitchy and raw, heading for the Carters' whenever she could because nothing ever changed there.

She'd always prided herself on being consistent, reliable, downright stalwart. She didn't want to ever be accused of being flaky or capricious. That was something that had driven her nuts about her own family, and she wouldn't be like that. Ever.

Van screwed her eyes shut and rubbed one of her bracelets. "It doesn't feel that way, though. I don't ever want people to think of me as feckless."

"I don't think anyone who's known you for more than five minutes could accuse you of being feckless. You give all the fecks, Van. All of them."

"Oh my god, calling you was a huge mistake." Even as she face-palmed, she was smiling. Nate's faith in her never failed to make her feel better.

"Feck you, I'm trying to help."

"If you were here right now, I'd smother you with a pillow."

"Fine, fine. I kid because I love you, but in all seriousness, you've never been inconstant a day in your life, and you wouldn't be starting now. You are a loyal person and considerate. It shows in everything you do, and I know it's important to you. I feel like the universe would give you a free pass on this.

"This is your life and your happiness we're talking about here. This isn't something you decided on a whim, and you're not going to leave anyone in the lurch. If you want out of academia, then get out. It's a damn hard job even if you love it and if you don't..." Nate sucked air between his teeth.

Everything he'd said was true. If she did leave—and that was still a big if—she'd fulfill her obligations first. She'd stay at the university through this year and speak to all the necessary people to figure out how to exit gracefully. She wouldn't leave holes in the class schedule, and she'd do her level best to find new homes for the few grad students she had.

"I understand what you're saying, and I'm not going to argue with you, but abandoning the investment of time and resources that have been poured into my brain... That feels wrong to me, Nate."

"I know it does. If you were a horrible and fickle person, you wouldn't give a feck. Sorry, couldn't help it. But you know that expression, 'Don't throw good money after bad'?"

Of course she did. "What about it?"

"Same principle applies here. Don't keep throwing more years of your life into something that makes you miserable just because you've already invested so much in it. Besides, it's not as though your education's going to be wasted. You might take some time off, do something that has nothing to do with your degree for a while, but you'd come back to it. You can't even help yourself."

For an engineer, Nate wasn't so dumb. "Fine. I'll think about it."

"Good call. Anything else you wanted to talk about? I get my cast off next week, but I'm dying here. Bored as feck."

If her stomach had been a tropical storm when she'd confessed her hatred of her job, it was a hurricane thinking about talking to Nate about Willa. Luckily, she wouldn't be dropping the bomb because Willa had already done that, but she was still queasy over what he might say to her about it. If he'd tried to warn Willa off, which it sounded like he might've, then maybe she'd been right and he was not at all thrilled about this.

"So here's the thing. It's possible I may have taken out how shitty I've been feeling about academia on Willa."

There was a pause, and Van considered the possibility Nate was rigging up his drone to come and assassinate her. Yep, totally possible.

"How precisely did you do that?"

The cautious tone of his voice made her stomach lurch. She hoped at least their many years of friendship would mean he'd murder her in some painless way. "I may have insinuated academia was for chumps and it would make her bitter and miserable."

"I see."

Jesus, could he put her out of her misery already?

"That was wrong and inexcusable, and it has far more to do with my personal feelings than it does with my belief in her abilities or her prospects. It might not have been a good choice for me, but that doesn't make it a bad choice for her."

"Uh-huh."

Was he biding his time until he could get a lock on her cell to determine her location? What was with all the minimal answers? Could he not yell at her and get it over with? She'd feel so much better if he would. Which was maybe why he wasn't, the canny asshat.

"Well?"

"Well, what?"

"Are you going to help me with this?"

"You want me to help you get back into my beloved baby sister's good graces in the hopes you'll also be getting back into her pants?"

Well, yeah, but... Eh, there was no sense in lying about it.

Nate knew. She could pretend she didn't know that he knew, but really, what would be the point? "Yes, okay. And what the hell did Willa actually tell you?"

"That you two had hooked up, but she made it sound like she was hoping for a lot more than that."

"And you didn't say anything?"

"Neither did you. Not even to ask my blessing before you got together."

"Go eat a bag of dicks, Natocracy Ulythaford Carter. If I'd asked your permission before I laid a hand on Willa, she would've punched me and I never would've gotten to kiss her."

"True. But my point stands."

He didn't sound upset, but Nate could seem cool on the outside and actually be a seething mess on the inside. Since he wasn't here, there was only one way to find out.

"Yeah, well, I was nervous about telling you. I rationalized putting it off by telling myself it was only a summer fling, but the thing is I...I want more than that. It just took me a while to figure that out."

There was unbearable silence from the other end of the line, and Van had to take up her fidget cube, bypassing all the other options and heading straight for the clicky bit. This part of the conversation required big guns.

"Look," he said finally, "as you've pointed out, it's not as though Willa is underage or terribly impressionable. And while I don't want to hear all the details, I'm totally fine with Willa having a sex life. She should. I'm not like those dudes who flip their shit when their best friend wants to be with their baby sister because honestly? If you're good enough to be my bestie, wouldn't it follow I'd think you were good enough for Willa too? And Willa's pretty great—of course you want more than just shacking up with her for a few weeks. But as smart as you are with books, you're less so with people and I was hoping she'd give you enough time to figure it out."

That was reassuring, but it didn't entirely squash all her worries so she cast her line again. "I wasn't sure how you'd feel about it."

She could practically hear Nate shrug. "Newsflash, Van. I think you're pretty great. My whole family does. As long as we can still have some time just the two of us doing our geek stuff, I'm good. Unless you hurt her, then I'll kill you."

That seemed completely reasonable. "Well, I have, but I'm prepared to make amends in any way necessary. I was hoping you'd have some suggestions because you usually do."

"Here's my advice: Tell her exactly what you told me and say you're sorry for fecking up. Tell her you want to be together beyond camp. Also, do something nice for her. Willa's not so into flowers and chocolates and stuff, but you know that. If you deserve her, you'll be able to think of something she'd like better than those generic things anyhow."

"Yeah, okay." Van could do that. She could apologize, sincerely, and with every expectation of having to grovel some because she'd been a giant turd blossom.

On the plus side, she'd spent the last five weeks getting a crash course on all the things Willa loved, from the expected—tennis and Molly Ringwald movies—to the less so—who would've thought a girl like that would want to look at rocks for her whole life or would be super-excited about *Star Wars* cosplay? "I can do that. And I should probably go so I can get to work."

"Fine. You better fix this, Van. Both of these things. Because if you don't, you're screwing my two favorite girls in the whole world, and I won't stand for that."

Usually she'd object to being called "his girl" because from most people she found it condescending and infantilizing, but she found it to be more affectionate coming from Nate. He sure as hell didn't mean it in a demeaning way, so she'd enjoy the fuzzy feeling of being acknowledged as one of his favorites.

She could do this. She could fix things with Willa, and she could get her career on the right path—a different one. In a methodical and responsible way, but one that would extricate her from this mistake she'd made and been too stubborn to give up on, even though it probably would've saved her some time if she'd come to this conclusion years ago. Oh, well. Nothing she could do about it until someone who wasn't her invented a time machine. In the meantime, she had some planning to do.

"I'll do my best. And Nate?"

"Yeah?"

"Feck off." Van hung up quickly, but not without hearing his snort of laughter first.

17

THE PINE NEEDLES CUSHIONED Willa's footfalls even as she pounded out her steps on the trail. Usually she loved running in the woods around camp, but at the moment, she was too upset to enjoy much of anything. She didn't even want to call Nate to talk about it, because despite his best efforts, there'd probably be a hint of *I told you so*.

Which, now that she'd run out some of her fury, she could admit might be fair. Nate had told her to take things slow with Van, and while she'd gotten defensive with him at the time and told him to shut his face because everything was great, she could see now he was trying to protect her. And Van.

If it took Van a couple of minutes to warm up to the idea of a hug, wouldn't it make sense that it would take her longer than that to come around to the idea of a relationship? It hadn't been fair of Willa to expect Van to magically read her mind and be on the same track to Girlfriends-ville.

She managed to elbow a tree branch out of the way before it whipped her in the face, but it scratched her forearm and burned a little. Much like the guilty feeling about having told Nate about her and Van. Yes, Van was a jerk for putting Nate's feelings above

Willa's, but she shouldn't have told Nate without at least giving Van a heads up that she was planning to.

Van and Nate had a far longer track record than she and Van did, and even if Willa didn't think Van had anything to worry about, that didn't give her the right to dismiss Van's concerns.

Willa dodged a rock on the trail, and when she came to the next fork in the path, took the long way around back to the cabins. Yes, she was calmer, but she wasn't calm by any stretch of the imagination, because even if she had fucked up, Van had still fucked up too, and didn't seem to realize it at all. Or if she did, she was more concerned with Willa having told Nate they were seeing each other. Which was not the point.

As much as she could look carefree, Willa had feelings, and Van needed to realize it and not just spew her own shit all over. Or if she wanted to spew, make it clear that it was *her* shit and not Willa's. Thus far, she had proved incapable of doing that, and no way could Willa deal with that for the long run. Which was maybe a moot point since it was possible there wasn't even a *present* for her and Van, never mind a future.

The idea was painful, more a deep throb of regret than the light sting her own misstep just now had caused her. She could and would apologize to Van for her shit communication skills, but she needed Van to take the first step. But would Van? As Willa felt the tears start to sneak up on her again, she pushed herself harder, trying to outpace the hurt.

———

WHEN WILLA GOT BACK from her run, she stalked through the cabin directly to the bathroom, not saying a word to Van and not even looking at her. Okay, totally deserved. Half an hour later, when she came out all freshly scrubbed and her hair pinned up in a braided bun at the crown of her head, she still didn't say anything to Van.

While Willa'd been out, Van had formulated a plan, one that would hopefully give her a second chance. So after Willa had plunked herself down on her bed, but before she could pull on her headphones, Van worked up the nerve to approach her.

"Hey."

"Hey." Willa didn't look up from the screen of her laptop. This was not promising, but Van was out of options. This was a last-ditch effort, and it had to succeed. It *had* to. Maybe she should start out slow and give a big speech, but she'd never been much good at that. Hopefully her actions would speak louder than her terrible, horrible words had.

Van swallowed hard, hoping that sick gurgly feeling in her stomach—like when she and Nate had downed way too much Pop Rocks and soda to prove your stomach would not in fact explode—would go away. It didn't, and it probably wouldn't unless she apologized. Even then, who knew if Willa would forgive her? She'd been a pretty big shithead.

"Wills," she begged. "Please. I know I fucked up and was completely unfair, and I want more than anything to make it up to you. The usual ways I know to tell someone I care…well, I feel like they wouldn't work for you. Not that you wouldn't appreciate the effort, but I want to do something you enjoy. And I think I found something. So pretty please with some ectoplasm on top? You can bash me in the face with your racquet—the crappy one, of course—if I'm lying."

Willa's face was pinched and wary, like she was worried Van was going to hurt her. Van hated it. So much. She deserved it, though, because she *had* hurt Willa. But she wouldn't do it again, not if she could help it. People screwed up all the time, of course, but she could at least make an offering. That's what she was trying to do, but she needed Willa to come with her.

"Just a couple of hours is all I'm asking. After that, if you never want to talk to me again, I won't bother you. Swear."

"Swear on Holtzmann?"

Ugh, these Carter siblings and their vendetta against her Holtzmann—what was with that? But if that was what it took, she was willing. "Yeah, I swear on Holtzmann."

"Fine, but this had better be good."

———

FORTY-FIVE MINUTES LATER, they were climbing out of Van's car, and whoo boy, did Willa have something to say about where they'd ended up.

"You seriously made me drive forty-five minutes to bring me to a gas station? Look, I don't know if this is the only place for miles that carries your preferred flavor of Mountain Dew or what, but you need to take me back to camp. I don't want to be here."

The air was cooling off from the high heat of the summer, and the breeze was gentle but carried a chill, bringing hints of fall and, well, urine, because they were at a sketchy ass gas station. What the hell? She'd had visions of Van bringing her out to some meadow where they could lie on a blanket in the grass, holding hands and then maybe making out while they were allegedly watching the stars or some sort of astronomical event Van had found out about. If a ratty old gas station was Van's idea of an apology, she was doing it wrong.

"It's not the gas station, promise. Come with me, please? Five minutes from here. Just five."

Willa blew out a breath from her nose, but god she wanted to take that chance, wanted to follow Van. Before yesterday, she would've followed Van anywhere and everywhere, but after her tirade about academia and her complete freak-out over Nate, her confidence in the woman she'd had a crush on for more than a dozen years had been shaken.

She considered the hand on offer and eventually took it. Van squeezed, and it nearly forced tears to the surface.

They walked to the back of the gas station, nodding at a grizzly-looking dude behind the counter on their way. Behind the squat cement building, there was a hill, and Van led her up a steep and narrow but well-worn path. True to her word, in about five minutes, they'd circled the hill and were standing so they could barely see the glow of the overhead lights from the gas station and none of the building itself.

That's when she saw it. A fissure in the side of the hill. It was rocky and narrow, but there. Van tugged her hand, and she followed, hope floating to the top of her well of feelings. Had she—

When they stepped through the tight opening, Willa could tell that, yeah, she had. Van had found her a cave.

"So turns out that, due to the composition of the bedrock around here, there aren't so many caverns. Too much metamorphic rock-like schist, not enough limestone." Van was using her professor voice, but she was looking around like a kid at Disney. "I know this isn't impressive compared to what you're used to, but I wanted to bring you here because it seemed like the right place to tell you something important."

"What's that?"

Van pulled Willa around until she was gripping both of Willa's hands in hers. "I'm sorry. For a few things, so give me a minute to get it all out. I'm sorry for putting my friendship with Nate above your feelings. Yeah, he's my best friend and losing that would crush me, but if I wasn't willing to be honest with him about it, I shouldn't have started this or let it get as far as it did. Your feelings are important to me too, Wills. If I had it to do over again,

I'd tell Nate straight up that I was interested in you from the beginning.

"Also, I let my own feelings about academia color what I said to you, and I shouldn't have. Your journey isn't the same as mine, and it would only make sense if we end up in different places. If you want to finish your PhD and apply for tenure-track positions, you absolutely should. Your passion, talent, and dedication would be a real asset to whatever university you ended up at, and I apologize for ever making you doubt that."

Willa's eyes watered, and her chin wavered. She was about to say something, but Van shook her head.

"I think I'm going to be leaving my job and looking for a position in the private sector because that's the right decision for me. I've actually been talking to one of the senior people at Aquitaine about going to work for them eventually, although I'm not going to make any decisions yet. What I will do is use any and all resources and connections at my disposal to help you get whatever job you want. If I know someone who knows someone, I will give them anything they want for you to have a chance at your dream."

"Even Holtzmann?" Willa was kidding, with her pathetic, tear-laden whisper, but it didn't sound like Van was when she answered.

"Even Holtzmann. I would give her up for you."

Which was the weirdest compliment Willa had ever gotten, but damn if it didn't make her feel good.

"I'd never ask you to give up Holtzmann. You love her. I don't see how giving her up would get me a job anyway, but I love that you offered. And I have my own apology to make. It wasn't cool of me to tell Nate about us without talking to you first. I got carried away because everything was so awesome that I assumed we both wanted to be together beyond camp. I shouldn't have made that presumption. But—" Willa bit her lip because she thought she knew the answer that would come, but she didn't want to make any more conjectures. That had not gone well for her. "But you do, right?"

"Yes, I do. It took me a while to admit it to myself because I can be kind of clueless, but yes. And I..." Van took a deep breath, looking like she'd chugged a whole glass of all the sodas mixed together. "I love you. I haven't said it, and I might not have done the greatest job of showing you, but I do."

Before Willa could cry—because she was totally gonna cry— she dropped Van's hands and reached out for her face, cupping her cheeks and brushing her thumbs over them. So soft. When she leaned in to kiss her, she knew her lips would be soft too. And hungry and warm, and if she could get her to...

Van moaned, and Willa took the opportunity to slide her tongue in between Van's lips, brush it against hers, and god, there was that spark that Van would probably make some adorable reference to. Willa wanted to get those references. Not because she suddenly had any strong desire to go to Comic-Con or be a devoted Trekkie, but it was important to Van and Van was important to her, and she could admit *Firefly* was actually pretty entertaining.

"I love you too, and I want you to be happy. We'll figure something out, okay? I want to be with you, and you know, they'll tell jokes about us—how many degrees does it take to change a lightbulb? They'll be funny, and I won't mind at all. Because I'll be with you, and you're pretty great when you're not trying to discourage me." Willa bit her lip, unsure of how much more to say. Did it really matter? Maybe it didn't matter now, but she knew Van was a big fan of having information. It was one of the things that made the world fit together like puzzle pieces in her perpetually logical way, whereas Willa was far more comfortable picturing the world as a Van Gogh painting in motion. So she gave Van another data point. "The thing is, everyone always treats me like Geologist Barbie because of the way I look and because, honestly, I'm not as smart as a lot of the other people in my program."

Van opened her mouth to protest, but Willa raised a hand. "No, it's true, and I'm not ashamed to admit it. I don't have as much raw intelligence as a lot of them. What I do have is the ability to work hard, and part of how I learned to do that was by busting my ass at tennis. So I don't regret any of it. I've gotten used to people underestimating me, but I never thought you'd be one of them."

Grimace was not a strong enough word for how pained Van's expression was. "I'm an utter shit, and I'll apologize as many times as you need me to. You are one of the hardest working people I know, and I'd be willing to wager my entire Wonder Woman collection you could do anything you put your mind to. I don't even have much in the way of an excuse for my behavior, except in a roundabout and completely wrong way, I was trying to protect you."

As much as that made her want to roll her eyes, Willa didn't. Van didn't like being wrong, and the fact she was apologizing so profusely—she might even call it a grovel—was enough. "You know I'm not a stupid kid anymore, right? You can't keep treating me like one."

Van touched a fingertip to Willa's nose. "You, my love, were never stupid. Nate and I did far more crazy shit than you ever did. As for being a kid, I'll probably catch some flack for having a younger, hotter girlfriend, but it's a sacrifice I'm willing and able to make."

At that, Willa did roll her eyes. "You still haven't said you'll respect my decisions."

"I will, I swear. Except when it comes to snack food. You're going to have to trust my judgment on that, okay? Because I can't even with this kale chip nonsense. And no one will ever convince me carob is even a distant relative of chocolate."

"Fine. You can be in charge of the snack cupboard. But I am going to make you eat quinoa."

Van wrinkled her nose, but then smiled. "Deal. Seal it with a kiss?"

As if there were any other way. Willa tipped her head to capture Van's mouth with her own, and it wasn't long before hands wandered and bodies pressed against each other. Then Van had the nerve to pull away. How dare she?

"Y'ever had sex in a cave?"

"What?" Willa smacked Van on the shoulder, which did nothing to dim her mischievous grin. "No. Caves are for working, not for...shenanigans."

"I thought geologists did it in the dirt?"

Willa groaned, and not with the pleasure Van usually inspired in her. "Oh my god, you and Nate make the worst puns in the whole world."

"Yeah, but you love us anyway."

"Yes, I do." To prove it, Willa kissed Van again, wrapping her arms around Van's ribcage and holding her so tight there couldn't be any air between them. With Van's body against hers, suddenly sex in a cave didn't sound like the worst idea. "Don't suppose you brought a blanket?"

18

"I HAVE TO ADMIT, I was skeptical, but you two totally pulled this off."

Heather beamed as she looked out over the boathouse. The Tullys had gone with a *Breakfast Club* theme—Heather was rocking a Claire Standish getup and had forced Michael into a John Bender outfit, complete with a tiny diamond stud that had to be a sticker. Michael loved Heather to the ends of the Earth and back, but Willa didn't think he'd go so far as to get an ear pierced for a party. Next to him, Willa slid Van an equally pleased look, although weighted probably less with earnest delight and more with I-want-to-jump-your-bones. Because Van looked even hotter than normal.

The John Hughes mash-up theme was proving to be an enormous hit. People from the Aquitaine session had taken up the gauntlet she and Van had thrown down. There were, of course, multiple representatives from *The Breakfast Club*, *Pretty in Pink*, and *Sixteen Candles*, but there were also people with fair-to-excellent imitations of *Weird Science* and *Uncle Buck*.

And Van...well, Van made an amazing Duckie. God knows where she'd found them, but she was rocking a blazer that looked eerily similar to the one Duckie wore in the prom scene of *Pretty in Pink* and a bolo tie. Seriously. Where in the Berkshires did one get a bolo tie?

Her own dress wasn't as good of a replica of Andie's pink monstrosity, but she didn't think Van minded she'd taken a few liberties. The halter neckline and bubblegum pink color were the same, but that was about where the resemblance stopped. Willa had gone for something more flattering—clingier than the original, and fuck no with the polka dots.

When Van smiled at her, looked at her in that way that she knew meant Van was picturing all the filthy things she was going to do to her later, she didn't think she could be happier.

The night was nearing its end, and so was the camp season. Hard to believe she had to go back to Stanford in a few days, all the way across the country from Van. But they'd text and email and Skype, and Van was going to come visit her. She'd promised, and that was something Willa could trust in. She'd watched Van be the best friend a person could ask for to Nate for her entire childhood, and loyalty was still one of the things Van did best.

After they attempted to shake their way through all the eighties hits, Van excused herself. Though Willa was bummed they'd likely miss the last dance, she couldn't blame her. The punch was pretty addicting stuff, and they'd both had several glasses. No wonder she needed to use the ladies' room.

Willa set to picking up some empty cups and abandoned paper plates, because they'd have enough to clean up once everyone had bunked down; she may as well get started now. The Aquitaine crew was pretty great, but neat as a pin they were not. Who was when they'd been downing Meg's punch all night?

That was when Otis Redding's "Tenderness" started to play. Willa loved that song and wished Van would hurry back so they could enjoy it together. But as she eyed the doors Van had disappeared through, damn if the woman didn't come busting through them, doing a pretty damn impressive imitation of Duckie in the record shop, serenading his not-so-secret crush.

It was epic to watch Van lipsync the whole thing, and Willa had to wonder when the hell she'd found the time to practice, but practice she must have because she nailed it. Totally fucking nailed it. Though the entire camp was gathered, watching Van get her enthusiastic groove on, Willa knew this performance was for her. Maybe later she'd give Van her own performance to show her exactly how grateful Willa was...

After the number was over, Van approached her—ruddy-faced, because that was probably the most physical activity Van had done all summer—and took her by the hands. "You know, I liked a lot of things about Duckie in *Pretty in Pink*, but one of the things I could never get my head around is he never told Andie how he felt. That and his 'nice guy' attitude." Van shivered, and Willa laughed. Yeah, she knew a lot of those guys. "So I'm going to be better than Duckie. I'm telling you now I love you, and I want to be with you. I'm making a promise out loud and with my whole heart."

Her Duckie was superbly swoon-worthy and she wanted to tell her so, but before she could, Van shook her head. "I will sort this out, and once I do, we will be together. The more I talk to Michelle from Aquitaine, the more I think they'd be a good fit for me, and know what the best part is?"

There could be a lot of things about Aquitaine Van was excited about. They clearly had excellent taste if they were trying to recruit Van and they'd had an eighties-themed retreat at a grown-up summer camp. Maybe they had cosplay Fridays or a desk decoration allowance? Willa didn't feel like guessing. "What?"

"They have offices in Palo Alto."

Not that she'd want Van to take a job because it was close to her, but the fact she thought that was the best part? Gave her the warm fuzzies. "That's literally next door to Stanford."

"Yeah, I know." Willa's heart swelled with the lopsided smile Van gave her, so she kissed her and kissed her again.

Van pulled away. "So if I end up working there, it'll be perfect. And if not, there are other places near there that do the kind of work I think I'd like to. Either way, we won't have to say goodbye at the end of the summer ever again. Promise."

THANK YOU!

Thanks for reading *In Her Court*. I hope you enjoyed it!

- If you'd like to know when my next book is available, you can sign up for my new-release mailing list at www.tamsenparker.com, follow me on Twitter at @TamsenParker, or Like my Facebook page at www.facebook.com/tamsenparker.
- Reviews help readers discover books. I appreciate all reviews and the time it takes to share your thoughts.
- You've just read the eighteenth book in the Camp Firefly Falls continuity. If you missed any from this season or 2016, you can find them all at http://campfireflyfalls.com. If you enjoyed Willa and Van, I hope you'll give some of my other books a try!

OTHER BOOKS BY TAMSEN

Looking for a Complication

(originally published as part of the *For the First Time* anthology)

Needs

(originally published as part of the *Winter Rain* anthology)

Anthologies

Winter Rain

Rogue Desire

Rogue Affair

ACKNOWLEDGMENTS

First, thank you so much to Gwen and Zoe for creating the wonderful world of Camp Firefly Falls and letting me be a part of it. I had so much fun setting Van and Willa's HEA against the backdrop you built. Thank you also to the entire CFF crew. I'd hang around a campfire with you all anytime.

Thanks also to AJ and Zoe for beta-reading my geek girls and appreciating all their dorkiness. Who wants to cosplay?

This book was written mostly during the month of November, aka NaNoWriMo. While I wasn't part of the official hoopla, I was definitely inspired by it, and all my friends who were participating.

I also wouldn't be able to maintain my sanity without my IRL crew: MTS, AJ, LG, EH. And thank you to my family for reminding me that there is a life outside my laptop. We'll have some great summer adventures of our own.

A very special thank you to MRF, whose career path partially inspired Van's, for making sure my computational biophysicist was spot on. You make me sound way smarter than I deserve, and someday you'll get to be Jason Bourne, I swear. Any remaining errors are mine.

To my editor, Christa, for whipping this book into shape—you earned your stripes on this one for sure. And my copy editor, Rebecca, who is my favorite CE—I can say that now! Also, my proofreaders, Christine and Michele, who dutifully read whatever I send them, and my cover artist, Lori Carter, who made my girls as cute on the outside as they are on the inside.

And last, but certainly not least, to my readers and reviewers: I hope you had a great time coming to Camp Firefly Falls and that you'll have fun exploring the rest of the stories in the continuity.

Made in the USA
Coppell, TX
16 March 2020